An Uprush of Mayhem

WITHDRAWN

JACK S. SCOTT

An Uprush of Mayhem

TICKNOR & FIELDS

NEW HAVEN AND NEW YORK

1982

Library of Congress Cataloging in Publication Data

Scott, Jack S.
An uprush of mayhem.

I. Title.
PR6069.C589U6 1982   813'.54   81-21298
ISBN 0-89919-095-2   AACR2

Printed in the United States of America

S 10 9 8 7 6 5 4 3 2 1

An Uprush of Mayhem

CHAPTER 1

She was a plain girl, and he was a handsome man. This is
why she was so excited. Nervous, even. Dates do not come
often to plain girls, especially with men so good-looking as
this. Not young, he wasn't exactly young. Thirty-five,
perhaps thirty-six. Much older than her few previous
dates had been; but then, young girls of her age — she was
eighteen — normally prefer the older man to swaggering
contemporaries who talk of nothing but football and their
mighty jousts with liquor, and are blatantly on the make.
Young girls fear young boys, being too self-defensively
absorbed to realize that the braggart swagger covers
insecurity to match their own.

She had spent hours on this, her day off, sitting at the
dressing-table in her little attic room, making up her
pale-skinned face and wiping everything off again. Silly,
that, with cosmetics the price they are; but she knew she
was plain, and was impelled as nervousness increased to
try for improvement. She bathed, and did not like her
thin, rather long body with its meagre breasts. Who
wants that lot? she thought. He won't. He must have had
much prettier ones. Will I be able to see, if I go without
my glasses?

But she was wearing her glasses when she met him,
yesterday evening. Sitting on a bench in the park, she
was; outwardly rather prim and self-contained; inwardly
aching with the almost tearful pressure of her unsatisfied
springtime sexual need, her deep, shy loneliness; and he
appeared.

She'd watched him, of course, his tallness coming
around the lake, and in her heart had made him her
lover, as all starved people — Hollywood depended upon

it—make lovers of the handsome unattainable; but not at all seeing him as within material possibility. And then he sat down, at the other end of the seat. After a while he smiled at her, spoke in a deep, warm voice. 'Lovely here, isn't it?'

Now she stepped down from the bus at the town terminus, freshly made up and auraed with the perfume her friend Mandy gave her for Christmas (Danger, it was called. The Key to New Horizons, according to the telly) and wearing her yellow dress. Her glasses, too, fearing she might fail to pick him out from the blur the world became when she took them off.

Not that he would turn up. Why should he? Prettier girls sat on park benches. Hunting girls, who would not let anything so gorgeous walk unattached for long. She'd wondered, very vaguely, that he should be alone last night; but caught in her own stirred need, her own new excitement, her impossible new horizons—soft words of love spoken in a deep, warm voice. His lips, his head to her breast, her small, shameful breast that he would love. Marriage? In white, and cutting the cake, and consummation—she jumped right over it. She'd never see him again, anyway. He wouldn't turn up.

But he did. He was there, smiling; putting a hand under her elbow to help her, unnecessarily but like a gentleman, down from the bus step; saying in that deep voice while her heart rose up hammering:

'Hallo. I didn't believe you'd come.'

She answered with a small shake in her voice. Shyness-stiffened face muscles made it hard to return his smile, but she did the best she could. 'I didn't think you would.'

'Didn't you?' he said. 'I've been waiting for it all day.'

So began her wonderful evening. He took her to dinner. Wine with it, and his deep voice saying things that made her laugh, more and more freely as the wine—she was not used to it—got to grips with her inhibitions. Sufficiently emboldened by it, as he poured her fourth glass she said:

'Why should a man like you want to got out with a girl like me?'

'How do you mean?' Lovely dark eyes he had, smiling at her over the table. Not a cheap restaurant, either.

'Well—you know.' She couldn't say outright: because you're so beautiful. She said it by implication. 'I'm—nothing. Am I? Glasses and all.' And my skinny body. 'I mean—you know. You must know plenty of girls.' And the slight—only slight—bow in my left leg.

He smiled, and he also had lovely teeth. 'It's not *girls*, is it? It's one *particular* girl. Somebody more than— well—just ordinary.'

She asked (wine is a fine emboldener) the inevitable question. 'Are you—married? Or anything?'

The fine eyes, turned serious, looked at her straightly. 'Divorced. Just came through.' Now his smile appeared again, lopsided. Suddenly he needed mothering. 'Very painful experience.'

'Oh.' A moment of silence. 'Have you got—did you have any children?'

Very soberly: 'No. Thank God for it.' And then, the shadow clearing, he laughed at her with his teeth, with his eyes. 'Drink up your wine before it gets cold.'

They looked in for a time at the Laughing Jackass, which is a discotheque; but it was one of those warm, soft springtime evenings that come sometimes between the snow and slush and bitter gales of a British winter and the rain and slush and bitter gales of summer. As he said, it was a sin to spend it indoors. She was glad to leave. Here was rampant nubility, bobbing unfettered up and down, rotating and thrusting sexually, expertly, under tight jeans or thigh-revealing frocks. No bobbing from her as

she hopped about awkwardly in front of his smooth un-
dulating, jealously aware of her plainness and by now
terrified of hungry competition, as a girl is always when
she falls with a bang into love. Girls with glorious breasts
were eyeing him already.

The obvious place to go, if you need to stroll under the
stars when you leave the Laughing Jackass, is into the
park—a lovely, big park of snug flowerbeds and wide-
open cricket and football pitches, of small woods—only
one, really, called baldly The Woods—and two ponds;
one small, where little boys sail boats; the other more of a
lake, tree-fringed and having an island, busy on fine
weekends with canoes and rowing-boats. It is called
Bishop Adam Park, after the nineteenth-century divine
who left it to the town in perpetuity. Died in a Soho
brothel, he did, clad only in his gaiters. But that is
another story, not noted on his marble tomb.

When they reached, all under the stars and moon, the
bench where he spoke to her yesterday, he said: 'Here it
is—where we met. Shall we sit down?' And soon after that
he kissed her, one hand moving to the nearest breast.

She pushed the hand away; broke breathless from his
lips to say: 'No—no—oh—no.' Not because she did not
want it, not because her whole soul and mind and body
were not melted into the great uprush of need for his
hands, his lips all over her, his wonderful body on hers;
but because most of what he was squeezing so gently was
foam rubber, and she didn't want him to know.

He knew, all right. A handsome man of thirty-five,
maybe six, if he has lived as this man lived has seized
upon them in all shapes and sizes, from those that are
virtually unbolstered nipples to those that are virtually
unnippled bolsters. He moved his hand downward, murmuring to soothe her—'There, my love—there—ah, my
love—'; to her belly, to her thighs and teasing upward;

while she moaned and gasped, mouth open to his tongue, feebly pushing at his skilful hand even while her legs opened. He whispered:

'Come on, my love—let's go into the woods.'

This area of trees and blackberry bushes—they never attain to a real crop, small boys eat them green—comes down to the lake. The bench where they were sitting stands almost in a clearing.

'Come on, my love,' he crooned. 'Come on—there's my love.' And with all the blood pounding in her, wet with need, torn by the virgin collision between desire and fear, she came almost sobbing to her feet.

Not long afterwards, she was dead.

CHAPTER 2

A black Anthony Eden hat stood in the area known as The Woods, above a battleship-grey raincoat. Beneath the coat, a serge suit, blue, with the double seat and the reinforced cuffs. Under the suit, the strangely apelike body of Detective-Inspector Alfred Stanley Rosher. Beside these things, in a nattier ensemble of grey suit, grey tie, grey trilby, grey coat, Detective Chief Superintendent (Percy) Fillimore gazed narrowly upon the world; and both men stood in silence. Nothing to say to each other, now or ever, God in His Infinite Wisdom having decreed them into the perfect personality clash.

It was raining. In the middle of that balmy spring night, quite suddenly, moon and stars were gobbled down by big and venomous black clouds, and teeming began. Two inches of it in Birmingham, flooding at Thames Ditton and three drowned near Mulbury Fotherham; which is far from either, so you can tell it was pretty widespread. Here, it had soaked the town, the countryside (FREAK STORM DESTROYS CROPS, the local paper said later. They keep the headline all made up, for use about four times a year) and Bishop Adam Park. None of these places, when rain falls upon the area, is likely to be missed.

Other men were here, of course. A veritable covey of coppers, some in uniform, others in plain clothes ranging from suits as sober, if not so durable—they don't make them any more—as Rosher's own, to scruffy anoraks and cagoules worn with boots more suited to cowboys, or soft-soled creepers, a far cry from the black beetle-crushers that made a plainclothes copper more copper than your standard copper, when worn with regulation raincoat and a bowler hat. Every man a specialist.

There were Scenes of Crime men sifting in the wet already, equipped with one of those neat small attaché cases inside which are tweezers and scissors and bottles and powders and measures and a pack of little plastic bags for hair and soil samples and fibres; and rubber gloves to ward off evil, and small sable brushes and puffs and pads and God knows what-all. Oh—and a magnifying glass, which policemen are reluctant to use because of mates who cry Sherlock and bystanders who titter. The case—they call it the Murder Bag—stood unopened as yet, nobody having found anything worth unsnapping the lock for. They were casting about, these men, within and without the roped-off dell at the four corners of which were uniformed, rain-caped constables, there to ensure that press and public, when they arrived, stood well back from the clue area, all around where the body lay. Actually, only the privileged would get this far.

The Chief Superintendent and his black-hatted hench-man stood within the roped dell, silently watching a short, plump, fussy pathologist who knelt beside the girl, having put down a piece of plastic first to save his trousers. Doctors, too, carry a bag, usually one of the soft-

bellied type called Gladstone, after a British Prime
Minister whose hobby was picking up prostitutes and
saving their souls. Probably the appellation Gladstone
Bag originally had a different connotation. This one, like
the Murder Bag, was not in use, it stood unopened beside
the owner. When the doctor grasped it by the handle in
his plump little hand and rose to his feet with it, and bent
over to pick up his plastic, the superintendent said:

'What do you make of it, Doctor?'

'Dead,' the doctor said. Statement of the utterly
obvious; but it is a fact that no policeman may assume a
body dead until a doctor has declared it so, though it be
lying here without a head. This was a belligerent little
doctor, a stander upon his rights; and to be the one who
officially starts the hounds baying is to possess a right.
Therefore, he said: 'Dead.'

'When?'

'About midnight. Or soon after. Strangulation.'

'Raped?'

'One assumes so. The undergarment is torn—the area
suggests it.'

Suggested it very strongly. The girl lay on her back
under the lately rigged canvas shelter, naked from the
waist down, pretty knickers around her ankles, pretty
skirt carefully pressed and donned for the date all rucked
up now and dark with rain; which had washed away any
surface traces that would have remained on a dry body.

'Strangled by hand, do you think?' Percy asked.

Immediately the doctor bridled, as if his professional
competence were being called into question. 'I'm not a
magician, you know, all I can do here is conduct a
preliminary examination. I'll make my full report when
I've had her on the slab.' He really was a tiresome little
man. And he wore a deerstalker hat. It didn't suit him.

'All right, Doctor. Thank you.' If there was snap in
Percy's voice it was not by particular intent. He knew the

little man well. The voice supplied with that narrow frame came with inbuilt snap, that's all. It showed from the very cradle. She had never, his mother always said as she dealt with his diapers, known a child like it. Mind you, she didn't know many. Discouraged, she never had another. Her son signalled now to men standing idle. They moved in, one setting the focal plane shutter of the big plate camera which many police photographers prefer still, for celery-crisp definition. Percy addressed the doctor again. 'I'll be down with her as soon as she can be moved.'

'I shall be there.' The doctor marched off, back to his car standing among police vehicles, Percy's black saloon and an ambulance at the park gate. Not a glance at Rosher. Didn't like Rosher, who in his Old Blubbergut days—which were here again, for sure—was wont to call him George, just to see the rich, port-fed blood rush to his ears. George was indeed his forename, it was one of the things he had to live with. Hated it; which fact Rosher had divined, and so spoke it with relish. It brought definite satisfaction to the doctor when they bust Rosher down. And now the damned monkey had been jacked up again.

One of the men bent over the body straightened, and came to fetch the Murder Bag. A scruffy man, but an inspector in his own right. Passing, he said to Percy: 'Pity about the rain. Washed a lot of stuff out.'

'Uh-huh,' said Percy. 'Can't be helped.' He settled to watch activities with his stomach churning. It always churned at the start of a case that would load his narrow shoulders with great responsibility. Here he stood again, in a wet wood; churning and wishing—he did it so often—that he had followed Uncle Albert's advice, and gone to work in a nice warm bank. Look at Uncle Albert, plump and happy, living out retirement in his centrally heated bungalow with a cut-glass decanter and an inscribed gold watch.

In time, the scruffy inspector said: 'All right, Mr Fillimore, she can go now;' and Percy nodded once more. Men moved forward with a stretcher, to inflict upon the girl the standard indignity that comes to the murderee before the final, monstrous indignity of post-mortem. They shoved her into a canvas sack, laid her on the stretcher and joggled her away, out from the bushes and along the path to the amublance. And only the heavens to weep.

Percy said to Detective-Inspector Rosher, as he resettled his grey trilby before leaving: 'All right, Mr Rosher. You know what to do.' And this is a needling thing to say to a long-service man even though a murder enquiry comes very seldom to a smallish town force—the last here came almost by accident, when two men were done to death by a motor caravan last summer; it sealed Rosher's re-elevation—has been through it all before.

But Rosher, even though he felt the needle, took no umbrage. Newly bounced up again from detective-sergeant, assured of full pension in a little over a year's time, aware of being already a legend in the force as the only man ever to come back from downgrading (he was, in fact, the only man ever downgraded. Coppers, whose business it is to study criminal methods, know pretty well how not to get caught), Old Blubbergut again and unchained from a CID room desk, his penchant for umbrage had noticeably slackened. A pendulum on the upswing late in life induces mellowing in a man. Not that Rosher would or could ever truly mellow; but where before the traumas his response to Percy would have been a savage interior 'Sod you, mate,' his interior response now was a mellow 'Sod you, mate.' Almost contemptuous; because Rosher now enjoyed the patronage of the Chief Constable, no less, and the old arch-enemy's fangs were cut off at the gum.

So he watched the DCS (it means Detective Chief

Superintendent) walk away in company with the
constable who was first on the scene and must stay close to
the body now until he guaranteed in court that this was
indeed the corpse to which he was called, and turned
when a thin, cadaverous man in a flat hat and knicker-
bockers approached with a dog at his heels and said:

'Er—excuse me—can I go home now? Only the wife'll
be wondering, see.'

This was the man who found the body. Taking the dog
for an early-morning walk—always do, winter and
summer, the wife'll tell you—and it ran into the bushes
and started barking. Ran into the bushes, see? Started
barking. So I went in and there she was. That's all I
know. 'Course I didn't touch her, not stupid, am I? Read
enough detective stories, the wife'll tell you.

The inspector surveyed him rather benignly. No harm
in him. Just little John Public, a bit flustered from doing
his duty and rather apprehensive, as people usually are,
face to face with a quantity of policemen. He said: 'I see
no reason why not, Mr—er—'

'Reckit,' the man said.

'Mr Reckit. We have your statement. Somebody'll call
on you to put it in writing, get you to sign it.'

'Sign it?' the man said. They do hate to sign anything.
In case it is used in evidence against them, presumably.
You could see this one wishing he'd tiptoed away, left the
body where it was lying.

Rosher grinned evilly within as he added: 'And we'll be
needing you for the inquest. You'll be notified, of course.'

'Inquest?' said Mr Reckit. 'I didn't do nothing. Only
found her, I don't know nothing about it. It was the dog,
I take him for a walk every morning regular, winter and
summer. Done it for years, the wife'll tell you. She'll have
me breakfast ready.'

'Nothing like a good breakfast,' Rosher said, 'to set you
up for the day. Thank you for your cooperation, sir. We'll

be in touch. Off you go, mustn't keep the little woman
waiting.'

'She won't like this,' said Mr Reckit. 'It'll play on her
nerves.' He left, with his dog, bound for where congealing
eggs and bacon awaited in 28 Lime Walk. There's not a
lime for miles around, it's a narrow council-house alley
bordered with morose and cunning privet.

Now approached the only real fly in Inspector Rosher's
new ointment. Percy, perhaps, could be categorized fly,
being the man who would direct, and in theory control,
Rosher's work on this new-come murder; but Percy was
the long-known irritant, so familiar as to be integral to
life as she is lived. This other fly was called Detective-
Sergeant Reginald Harold Boggis, transferred not long
ago from CID in the big city. He would function on this
case as assistant in the field to Inspector Rosher; and
Rosher misliked him. Saw him as a bombastic, rock-
skulled, insensitive, ham-fisted, flat-footed copper.
Which is precisely how many people saw Rosher.

'Weather hasn't done us any favours,' the sergeant said
as he came to halt beside his superior. You'd have
thought he was equal at least. More equal than many.
City policemen of whatever rank very often adopt this
attitude towards their small-town cousins. God, how it
rankles. 'Blotted everything out.'

'Hmph,' said Inspector Rosher. They might have been
taken for father and son, standing together like this. The
same long-bodied, bandy-legged burliness, the same
thick-necked, bullet-headed look. The same short-back-
and-sides haircut not entirely hidden by the black hat
riding low upon the older man's brow, the waterproof
pork-pie on the other. Facially, however, they differed.
Where Rosher bore a startling resemblance to a gorilla,
the man Boggis had a good deal of hippo about him,
reinforced with the bulldog's underslung jaw.

He spoke again. 'Going to organize house-to-house?'

There are people born into the world so similar in type that they automatically abrade. This was exactly the sort of question that Rosher himself had framed often. On the receiving end, he felt the prick of irritation familiar to many of his own superiors. Of course he would initiate house-to-house, and all the other routine activities that go with the beginning of a murder hunt. He was coppering before this bomb-headed bastard came up. Aye—and not poncing about sticking tickets on double-line parkers in the bloody city. To evade answer he whipped out his handkerchief and blew a blast that echoed through the wood. Strong men jerked, their concentration shattered.

'Bloody hell,' said Sergeant Boggis admiringly. 'You can go a bit, can't you, on the old hooter?'

Rosher wiped up and stowed the handkerchief. He coughed. Tilted the black hat to scratch with a thick forefinger the tenpenny-piece tonsure set on the crown of his durable skull. 'You stick around here,' he said. 'I'm going back to the station. Anything turns up, get on the blower.' He turned, and his bandy legs walked him away.

There it is again, you see. Provocation. Sergeant Boggis watched him go, and he thought: What do you think I am, a bloody idiot? Of course I'll get on the blower if anything turns up. Not likely to sit in a corner crooning over it, am I? We're not all bloody hicks. Why they ever bumped you up again I shall never know. Ought to have put you out of your misery, let a younger man have a go.

Ah well. So it was, is now and ever shall be.

CHAPTER 3

It did not take long to start the ball rolling and for it to pick up useful matter. Before Percy returned from the post-mortem—most chief investigating officers attend the post-mortem, in case things turn up which the pathologist may dismiss or eliminate, but which deserve close attention—the teams were out, calling house-to-house; asking if anybody had seen a girl, alone or with a man, pass this way last night. Before midnight. Girl with glasses, five feet four, wearing a yellow suit. Nobody in any of the houses close to the park said they had, but this brought no disappointment. People rarely remember anything about anything, confronted suddenly by knocking policemen. Later, having had time to mull, somebody might ring the station. So the copper knocks and plods on, expecting nothing and usually getting it.

Other things were happening, too, of course. Forensic was at work, the lads were still in the dell, the press as ever was a pain in the posterior, the rubbernecks were rolling up and complaining bitterly when they were stopped at the park gates. Rosher, given access to the girl's clothing, had spent time on the telephone and gone again in a hurry, taking with him a constable more temperamentally suited to be dogsbody than was Sergeant Boggis, successfully shaken off and still awaiting developments at the dell.

Rosher's initial problem: to establish identity. Not difficult, usually. A woman's handbag contains indentifying matter. But if this girl carried a handbag, it was missing; which meant, since no worried mother had come seeking, a check through fingerprints in case she had a record; tooth inspection to enable checks by dentists through their files, examination for identifiable scars and so on; and laundry marks. Rosher had been phoning laundries.

He was lucky. Hit it first time. Well, of course, there are not too many laundries in the town. The suit had come for cleaning to Acme Steam Ltd. from the fine house owned and lived in by Sir Roland Goyt. At which news the inspector reached for his hat and left with

alacrity, pausing only to coopt the young constable and to
tell Sergeant Barney Dancey, that benign man who spent
his duty hours contentedly cooped behind the glass
window of the booth marked Enquiries, where he was
going. He carried with him photographs. Another
advantage built into the plate camera: it does not take
long for a motor-cyclist to rush the operator's first shots
back to the station in their slides, where they can be
developed individually and printed wet. A good team will
give you prints in a few minutes flat.

Whatever tiny pins had been pricked into the
inspector's mind were fallen out now and forgotten. He
sat beside the driver-constable on the journey through
town to the salubrious outskirts where the few houses
stand separate in private parkland looking down their
noses at each other, enjoying his twitching antennae and
wondering with a good feel in his gut if his newly risen
star was about to zoom up and spatter like a rocket.
Because:

Sir Roland Goyt. This was an old buzzard under
investigation already, by police, Inland Revenue,
Customs and Excise and you name it. From this house
had come the load of assorted goodies found to be in a
hijacked van, the driver of which, one Eddie Langdon,
was rocked to sleep by Rosher's mighty hammer—it was
this that clinched the re-elevation—before he had a
chance to draw his gun. Which Rosher didn't know he
possessed, when he unleashed in righteous wrath that
wicked right fist.

My God, the stuff in there! Gold and silver bullion,
masterpieces by Masters both Old and New. An
illuminated medieval Bible stolen long ago from
Winchester Cathedral—they were touchingly two-tailed
at seeing it again. But they couldn't have it yet, the law
was still at work—and even that beautiful Saxon
drinking-bowl, adrift from the Waverley Hoard.

Diamonds? One of 137 carats, that's all, besides many another. Rubies—emeralds—the bosom upon which the lot could nestle would need to be big as a cumulus cloud.

So where did it all come from? And where were the records of purchases and taxes paid and Customs clearances and duties and the like? And what else was in that house?

Awkward questions. Sir Roland took to his bed, as wizened and shattered a little armaments multi-millionaire as ever drew nigh to his last breath; while very clever lawyers—money will buy you anything, and even this little man knew that he must spend now, in spite of the agony it caused—fought with writ and counterwrit and all the low cunning of their kind to block entry into the house. Which, this far, they had done since the back end of last summer. Sir Roland had not even been interviewed in person. Money will also buy you a doctor skilled in dramatic interpretation.

Well, then: if the old sod tied in somehow with the murdered girl, in went the police—and Rosher first, right now. You can't keep a murder enquiry out. This could be big. This could be great, fat kudos. Which is why he was here, well on the way without a word to Percy. Percy, the bastard, raised by radio or telephone, would undoubtedly have said to hell with the post-mortem and shot along here himself. So Rosher clipped the book. Safely enough, he knew a deal about the book and where a man could reasonably clip. He'd left word with Barney, and a detective on a murder case must be expected to be here, there and everywhere, scudding about like Sonja Henie. A skating film-star, she was, and one of the lusts of his youth.

He stood under a solid, pseudo-Gothic porch in front of the Norman-style oak door of this noble pile, then, and rang a chiming bell, with the car in the drive, his witness constable beside him and something like happy excitement pleasuring the underbelly. At second ringing the door was opened by a squarish lady who might have been younger, and who had obviously paused before answering to claw the metal curlers out of her greying hair, since one hung from a frond above her left ear. Because this was not the sort of house where a woman appears in a bedraggled washing-up pinny, frowsy slippers on her feet and a fag in the corner of her mouth. It was indeed a noble pile, designed as one by the eminent Victorian, Sir Gilbert Scott, who set up St Pancras station along similar lines.

The lady said: 'Yes?'

Off came Rosher's black hat in one practised snatch as he bared alarming teeth in the beige beam which, he was convinced, steeped him in charm. His initial approach always, applied particularly to the member of the public who chanced to be female. He spoke winningly, all the vowels mangled in the style favoured by operators on telephones, and girls in supermarkets when they use the intercom to tell Mr Gumble he is wanted in the front office. The constable looked at him with surprise.

'Ah. Good morning, madam. Mrs—?'

'Rummidge,' the lady said. The clutching curler gave up, and fell with a small clatter on to the parquet at her feet. Deftly she kicked it sideways, out of sight under the door. Didn't even look down to do it.

'Mrs Rummidge. How do you do. We are the police.' Unnecessary identification, the constable was in uniform; but it comes automatically as the card is briefly flashed. 'Detective-Inspector Rosher.'

'Ah,' said the lady. 'I've told you before, I don't know nothing about nothing, I'm only the cook. Well—cook-housekeeper, really.'

'Not me, madam.' Almost coy, the winning manner. Terrified many people, it was like being suddenly confronted with a playful gorilla. 'You didn't tell me, this is my first visit. May we step in?'

'Well,' said the lady, 'I don't know. I don't answer the door, really, it's not my job. Sir Roland's give strict instructions—'

But Rosher was in. An irresolute lady cannot hold a door against an onward-bound policeman. She falls back, and he has ways of converting a small door-gap into a big one without so much as touching anything; and there he is, inside. Both, if there are two of them.

The one like a great ape now said: 'We won't keep you long, madam.'

'He'll be wanting his breakfast,' Mrs Rummidge said.

'You'll be giving it to him before it's even cooled.'

'It won't do that,' she said. 'It's only prunes.'

'Ah.'

'It's all he can take, really.' 'He' would be Sir Roland.

'Do you have a young lady working here?'

'No. Not a young lady, no.'

'A girl,' said the constable. 'A young girl.' And Rosher achieved the very difficult feat of squirting a snarl at him out of the corner of his eye.

'Only Evie. She ought to answer the door, really. Only she hasn't been in all night.'

'Ah,' said Rosher. His little beaming eyes had shot around. Nothing here in the furniture line to suggest priceless antiques, no pictures on the wall, not even a carpet on the parquet floor. Well, whatever the old buzzard had left he wouldn't hang it in the hall for clear sighting by any copper or tax-man or quivering Customs and Excise wallah who got as far as the door. Stained-glass windows on each side, even if the bolts shot home at his approach. Take a look further in. Already moving, he said: 'Shall we just go into the drawing-room?'

'Well—' said Mrs Rummidge, 'Sir Roland—'

Too late. Bandily, he was already crossing the hall. Even the constable was left standing. He caught up, and so did the lady, just as the inspector's hairy hand reached for the knob of one of several doors set around the big hall. He opened this door and walked into a broom closet. 'Ho, ho, ho,' he said. 'Silly me.'

'It's—it's the next one,' Mrs Rummidge told him, in a voice that twisted its hands together. 'Sir Roland give strict instructions—'

'I have no doubt Sir Roland would wish you to give us your full cooperation, madam.' Rosher eased the photographs, still tacky, out from the plastic envelope. Nothing in this room, either, looked all that valuable. Except the room itself, big and airy and french-windowed to the well-tended garden. You don't buy these great, hand-tooled houses with Co-op stamps. 'This girl we were speaking about. Does she look like this?'

'Oo-er,' said Mrs Rummidge. 'What's happened to her?'

The beam faded from Rosher's simian features, displaced by a grimness about the mouth, a hardness in the little eyes. 'Murdered, madam. This one's been murdered. Is she yours?'

'Oh my God!' Mrs Rummidge put a hand to a heart too far buried under bosom to feel the benefit. 'Oh my God! Poor little thing. Poor little Evie. Oh my God!'

'Perhaps you'd care to sit down. I have to ask you a few questions, I'm afraid. Constable—sort out the kitchen, fetch a glass of water.'

'It's all right,' said Mrs Rummidge, and sat heavily in an armchair. Her knickers came down to the knee. 'It's— only the—shock. Seeing her—like that—' She closed her knees together; pulled her skirt over them.

'When you're ready, then, madam. Take your time.'

'Yes. Yes,' the lady said. 'Yes. Yes. Oh, poor little thing.'

She was Evie—or Eva—Brewster, aged 18. Living-in maid here for more than a year. Went out last night—

excited all day. Date, she said. No, she didn't have many. Any. Well—she's not pretty or anything like that, is she, poor little thing! *Wasn't* pretty, although you could hardly believe it. Her being murdered. I mean, you don't expect it, do you? Only what you read in the papers.

No—the man didn't call for her. She met him in town, caught the six o'clock bus. No, I don't know where. No, she didn't say where they were going. She said he was like a film star, but whether he was or not I couldn't say. I mean, if you ain't used to that sort of thing—you know, if you're lonely, like—anybody who whistles at you can look like a film star, can't they? I'm not being funny, like, poor little thing, but—well—you know.

Mrs Rummidge was warming to the work. Women always do.

Well—yes—I reckon she must have been lonely. Read a lot of Mills and Boon. Not that there's any harm in it, I've read a few myself—well, the telly's not up to much, is it?—but not like she did. No, she didn't seem to have no friends, kept herself very much to herself as they say. No—no relatives as I know of. Not close ones, she came here from an orphanage. Bromley way, or somewhere. Or was it Birmingham? Good little worker, she was. She should have answered the door to you, really, but of course she hasn't been home all night.

When Rosher had entered all the notes he needed into his little black book he stemmed the flow. 'I shall need to see her room, of course. And somebody will be calling to collect her things.' He wouldn't do it himself. The somebody would probably be a somebody who had been trying to get in for months.

'Oh,' she said. 'Ah. I don't think Sir Roland—'

Rosher spoke crisply now. Second stage of his technique. It could move on from here to pulverizing, if the subject became obstructive. 'We are investigating a murder, madam.'

'Ah,' she said. 'Ah. Mm.'

On the way up the handsome stairs, and on up others less handsome, the inspector asked: 'Did she have a handbag with her, do you know?'

'I expect so. She always did when she went out. Everybody does, don't they?'

'Mm,' said Rosher. He didn't.

'Black plastic, hers was. The one she usually carried, anyway.'

The girl had lived in an attic room, one of several that would have been stuffed with servants once, in the good old times when they devotedly worked an eighteen-hour day with church twice on Sundays for humpence a year and two uniforms, weeping when they were drummed out because the master, or son, or both, had put them in the family way. Only this room now was open; and inside were the pitiful bottles and beautifying jars just where she left them, and mules under the dressing-table, and frocks in the wardrobe. Cheap mock-tortoise toilet set, cheap mock-leather manicure case. In the drawers—Rosher looked. He bandied about prying into everything—clean underwear neatly folded and two or three blouses, a pair of jeans, odds and ends. As he pried, he asked a question now and again.

'Were you worried when she didn't come home?'

'I didn't know. Not till this morning, she had her own key.'

'Were you worried this morning?'

'No, Not really. I mean, if he looked like she said he did—' She giggled.

Nothing much here. No note from the man or anything. If she'd been out with him before—she could have been—Forensic might tweezer something out. Hairs—fibres—dust. Something. He asked another question.

'Are you the whole staff?'

'Living in, yes. There used to be two more, but they
went. Just us and the gardener, but he lives in the cottage.
And he has a woman every day.'

'Does he? Strong lad, is he?'

'Who? Oh—' She giggled again. 'I mean Sir
Roland—he has a woman comes in every day, does the
rough work.'

'Ah.' No letters. Nothing. Might as well press on.
'Well—thank you, Mrs Gummidge, you've been most
helpful. We'll leave you now, you can serve up the
prunes, eh?' On with the charm again.

She simpered, emboldened by what she interpreted as
his naughty little joke. Actually, preoccupied by his
peering into drawers and things, he genuinely misunder-
stood. 'Keeps him regular. Ten o'clock in the morning,
you can set your watch by him.'

As they left the attic, Rosher asked: 'What's in these
other rooms?'

'Only bits and pieces,' Mrs Rummidge told him.

'Do you have keys?'

'Yes. Only we don't use them.'

'I'll take a look, if you'll fetch them.' Might as well grab
whatever was going. A lot of people stash a lot of stuff in
attics.

There was nothing remarkable in these attics. Plenty of
dust and cobwebs, naturally. Most of the boxy little
rooms were furnished still with cheap truckle-beds and
mean wardrobes, some with basin and ewer standing on
the deal washstand just as they were when the staff, made
redundant by a changing social order, picked up their
fibre suitcases many years ago and departed to sign on at
the Labour Exchange. Rosher would have liked very
much to prowl about the downstairs rooms; but even he
drew back from this. Cookie here undoubtedly would
report everything to Sir Roland; and Sir Roland's
reputation as a crafty old get was justly awarded. His

expensive legal buzzards would feast upon raw meat, and most of it from Rosher's carcase if he did the place over without a warrant. He could justify it—perhaps—by pleading that a murder enquirer is empowered to open many doors; but he'd had enough of disciplinary boards. He was up again, enjoying top-brass patronage. Think of the past, think of the pension, and leave it.

So he thanked the lady once again, and she saw them off the premises with enormous relief. The rain had stopped, the sky was pushing the clouds apart. Under the Gothic porch, Rosher replaced his hat; presumably so that he could snatch it off again, since he immediately did. The telephone-tone came back now, buoyantly floating on joviality like a malformed waterlily. 'Well—thank you once again, Mrs Gummidge. One could wish everybody were so cooperative. Good morning.'

'Good morning, Mr Nosher,' she said. 'It's Rummidge, really. With an ah.'

The parklike expanse of the grounds looked well under sunshine dappling it through the torn cloud-curtain. No obtrusive din here. Only the twitter of birds, and the chatter of a motor-mower piloted by a whiskery man over the green and billiard-table-surfaced lawn. A sobering thought: if you have lived all your life by mass murder and amassed a mighty competence, though you be under investigation from every quarter and proved to the hilt bent in all directions, you are the man who will get his lawn cut, while honest citizens toil through Sunday. The radio was squawking as they approached the car. 'Car 4F. Four-r-r EFF,' it said. 'Come in, Four-r-r Foxtrot. Over.' The young constable said, boyishly pleased that in the whole wide world he and he alone had been singled out:

'That's me.'

Rosher grunted. Opened the car door, inserted himself

and picked up the microphone. 'Car 4F,' he said. 'Over.'

'Hallo 4F, hallo 4F,' the little set squawked. 'Where the bloody hell you been? Over.'

'Hallo, HQ,' said Rosher. 'Detective-Inspector Rosher speaking. Over.'

'Oh Christ,' said the little machine. 'Sorry, I thought it was Tony Noakes. The super wants a word. Hang on a minute.'

A moment or two of static and Percy's snap came through, scaled down but not diminished. 'Mr Rosher? Where are you?'

'Just leaving Notley House. Sir Roland Goyt's place.'

'Why was I not notified that you were going there?'

That was a smile tugging at the edges of Rosher's thick lips. 'Thought you were busy. I left word with Barney.'

'I trust,' Percy snapped, 'that we are not about to pursue our own courses, regardless.' The significance of the visit had not escaped him, obviously.

'*I'm* not,' said Rosher. I don't know about you, the tone implied.

'What have you found out?'

Rosher told him. Name: Evie—or Eva—Brewster. Age 18. Orphan, from Bromley. Or Birmingham, investigation should reveal which. And so on. When he finished, Percy said:

'She was strangled. Sexual intercourse had been committed, we have samples of semen. Since you're where you are, I suggest that you call in to the Canton Restaurant on the way back. Contents of the stomach suggest Chinese food, consumed not long before death. With wine.' No idiot, Percy. A man does not really attain high rank and hold it upon bull alone, whatever Rosher would have told you with regard to the foe under review. Very good detective, actually. Not that he displayed here any kind of brilliant deduction. Only the Canton, of the three Chinese restaurants in the town, was liquor-licensed. Fair bet that the wine was drunk there and not separately, in a pub. Or the handsome man's flat? Handsome men usually have a flat.

'Right,' said Rosher. 'I'll get on to it. Anything else?'

'That's all,' Percy snapped; and he clicked them asunder without so much as an over and out.

A few minutes later Rosher stood with his acolyte in the Canton Restaurant, talking to the proprietor and a sleek-haired, eternally grinning wee yellow waiter who remembered the girl well, and her companion too. A tall man. Velly high, the waiter said at first, and Rosher thought he meant the man was drunk until a yellow hand stretched up to measure six feet or so from the floor. Pressed for fuller details, the little man proved vague; mainly because he lacked command of English ('Dark or fair?' Rosher asked. 'Yes,' said the waiter, all toothy grin and enthusiastic nodding) and partly, perhaps, because to the Chinese all Occidentals look alike. So the inspector took him down to the station tucked into the back of the car, which he seemed to enjoy very much; and here he chortled for an hour over mug shots of all the known villains in the town, with particular emphasis upon the violent and sexually bent. After which they brought out the Identikit bits and pieces.

All this while, of course, other people were working. House-to-house and Forensic teams, those Scenes of Crime men still in the dell; and others by now equipped with photographs, calling at pubs and clubs and wherever a man is likely to take a girl on a Saturday night. Sunday is, it goes without saying, an awkward day for this kind of thing. Nobody is working, people have to be tracked home, where late toilers incline to be still in bed. The Laughing Jackass people were visited, as routine; but lighting in there is dim, and one jumping, gyrating couple is very like another; and the doorman, who must have admitted them, was so stoned on LSD last night—mind you, he kept very quiet about it—that he didn't remember anything or anybody. So he simply said no, he hadn't seen her Saturday or ever.

Nothing much was coming in, then, but no fret was caused thereby; except perhaps to Percy, who fretted automatically and had the stomach to prove it. Policemen hope a case will roll itself up before their gratified eyes as soon as they prod; but they never expect that it will. Wherefore, there was no particular tension in the panelled room with the haircord carpet and an unrestricted view of the parking lot where the Chief Constable, current in the line of incumbents, stood with his chief henchmen and studied the Identikit offering. Percy was here, and Rosher; and Detective-Sergeant Boggis, back from the park. Also present: Chief Superintendent Rolly Rawlins, head of the uniform branch and not unpopular with his men in spite of it.

The Chief Constable said: 'I don't know. I really do not know. I suppose these things are of some use, but I really don't know. If he looks like this, you certainly wouldn't call him handsome, would you? More like a gorilla than anything.' All minds flashed to Rosher. He alone remained unconnected. We do not see ourselves when we confront a mirror, we see what we think we see; and Rosher was not tuned in to seeing himself as gorilla. Conscious of balancing on the fragile rim of *faux pas*, the Chief added hastily: 'Nothing wrong with gorillas, of course. But nobody, surely, ever looked like these things look?'

Percy spoke, testily. Even addressing his Chief Constable, a Detective Chief Superintendent can do this, provided he chooses the right Chief Constable and keeps it within reason. The lion-headed old bugger before this one would never have stood for it; but the old order changeth. 'This is how the Chinaman fitted it up, sir.'

Under Percy's personal eye. Criticism, therefore, came home to Percy.

'Oh, I don't doubt it, I don't doubt it,' said the Chief. 'Nobody's to blame, it's the machine. Or maybe the Chinaman.' And he smiled upon all, to show that he meant no offence. 'Well—get it out to the Press. Good work, to have anything at all so soon. Early enough to catch the television and tomorrow's papers. Pity there are no evening papers on a Sunday. Well done.' A Force works best, this Chief believed, when firm discipline is sweetened with encouragement. The old one believed in kicking its arse. Oh, how he kicked Rosher's.

The Chief handed the picture to Percy. It was vulgar without being funny. By Chinaman's selection, the man they were seeking had a violently receding forehead topped with coconut-tuft hair, little piggy eyes closer together even than Percy's, thick blubber lips and a chin like a concrete mounting-block. Not much of the gorilla about him, in truth, but a good deal of moron. A girl would be hungry indeed even to remain in a bus queue with him. Percy did not glance at it, he'd seen it before. He handed it to Rosher; who handed it to Sergeant Boggis; who, having no one to hand it to, took it away himself, okayed for the Press.

'Right, gentlemen,' said the Chief Constable. 'Let us go through it all again, shall we? So far, thanks largely to the efforts of Mr Rosher, we have made very fair progress, even obtaining the right to enter the house . . .' He spoke on; while Percy thought: The efforts of Mr Rosher? What's he done outside basic routine? Any competent beat-basher would have done as much, without expecting to be elevated to Golden Boy.

The Chief was finishing: 'Yes. Well—thank you, gentlemen. Pity about the rain, but we can't do anything about that. I'm sure we can crack this one without needing to call the Yard. We'll have a jolly good try, anyway, eh? Anything they can do, we can do better, eh? What do you say, Mr Rosher?'

'Eh?' said Rosher. 'Oh. Yes. Mm. Absolutely.' And in response to the Chief's encouraging smile he hauled back a thick upper lip to bare his brownstone teeth. After all, he owed this man. This man it was who dug him out of his grave and put him back in the land of the living, his own office in it and all, when Chief Inspector John (Bonker) Barclay retired and made a hole to squeeze him through. Not for him, then, to grunt and cavil if the old man chose to talk like a twat of a Boy Scout leader. We all have our faults, especially Chief Constables. This one was speaking again.

'Not much to go on, but we'll soon winkle the fellow out, no doubt. Pity we haven't got the handbag, it could have told us a lot. However, one expects it will turn up.'

And now Rosher did a clever thing. Although, examined closely, not all that clever. It's the sort of thing any detective must think of; if Percy had not done so yet it was because his mind was approaching the case from a different angle. Rosher garnered himself another small accolade. He said: 'Wine comes in bottles.'

'And bottles,' the Chief said approvingly—the trained mind strikes like a black mamba—'are perfect surfaces for prints. And a man pours wine for the lady. Well done, Mr Rosher. Well done, indeed. Last night's bottles should be still at the restaurant, they won't be cleared on a Sunday. Well done.'

It shows how different two men can be. The old Chief Constable would have been demanding to know why Rosher did not think of bottles and impound all the empties while he was at the restaurant. So, for that matter, would Percy.

In an exceedingly desirable apartment in the big city, which is not all that far from the town, a middle-sized but

muscular and very smartly tailored man named Leonard
Figgis paced about the living-room, as was his habit when
disturbed, or angry, or needing to think. Friends were
with him, business associates sitting in his elegant Swedish
chairs. There was Bernie Stephens, who had a lazy eye;
and James (Horsehead) Rumblelow. Also Eric, called
Bottle, Bowen and Charlie Palkin; normally designated
That Bastard, but only behind his back or in the secret
head. Upon a table made from frosted glass and chromed
steel in a style only a Swede would think of stood a
television set, newly switched off after the news flash that
brought shock.

Leonard, as he paced, was saying: 'So what's the silly
sod think he's up to? He's supposed to jolly her along, not
knock her off.'

James (Horsehead) Rumblelow, who was a bit dim,
said: 'It's not him, though, is it? I mean—that wadden
him.' He was referring to the Identikit picture of a
coconut-tufted, close-eyed, slab-jawed moron lately
spread over the television screen.

'Twat,' said Leonard. 'It's *her*, ain't it? It's the bird.
Ain't it?'

'I never seen no bird looks like that,' said Horsehead.

Bernie Stephens was brighter, but still not likely to
qualify as Brain of the Year. 'Might not be. Might be a
different one.'

'Don't be foggen stupid. Evie Brewster. Right? Maid.
Sir Roland foggen Goyt's maid. Said her name was Evie,
didn't he? Who else is it going to be?'

'That wadden him, though,' Horsehead said
stubbornly. A great big man, not one quarter so elegant
as the chair he sat in. 'He doan look nuffin like that.'

'Oh, for Chrissake!' Leonard raised his eyes to a ceiling
coloured to tone with his genuine Chinese carpet, his
Lincrustaed walls. 'The one they put out after the Post
Office at Cheltenham wasn't like you, was it? But you got

five years. They're *never* like nobody.'

'Bleeding liberty, that was,' said Horsehead. 'Looked like bleeding Dracula. 'Course, I was wearing a stocking-mask.'

Charlie Palkin spoke. Better brain altogether. Vicious, though, that was his trouble. 'Maybe we're over-reacting. He must have had plenty of women. I mean, he shouldn't be that hard up for a bit, should he, looking like he does? Why would he knock her off?'

'How the bloody hell do I know?' Leonard snarled. 'Don't know all that much about him, do we? He might have done half a dozen. Neville bloody Heath didn't look like it, did he? And look what he done. That's the bird, anyway, annit? Puts him right in the shit, then, don't it?'

A girl came through the door that led to bedroom, bathroom and the usual offices. A very nubile blonde, impressive breasts quivering beneath a short silk dressing-jacket that finished a long way from the floor. Leonard's latest playmate, and fit for a centrefold. 'Is it a private party?' she pretty-lisped, with a flapping of lashes. 'Or can little Mandy join in?'

'Sod off," said Leonard.

'Charming,' the girl said, all the lisp gone. 'Sod you, too, mate.' She turned and flounced back through the door. When she whirled the jacket hem went up to show a flash of delicate cheek above those long, long legs. All eyes but Leonard's riveted with an almost audible click. Leonard had preoccupations. Besides, he'd seen it all before.

When she had vanished and the eyes were loosed, Charlie Palkin spoke again: 'I still don't see why he'd knock her off. Easy, he said, didn't he? He reckoned she was panting for it. He wasn't even out with her for his oats, was he?'

'Go bloody mad when they're on the job,' said Leonard, 'don't they, some of 'em? Heath did. Look at

Christie—used to bleeding strangle 'em.'

'She was bleeding strangled, wadden she?' Horsehead
again. 'Doan see what they get out of it, meself. I like it
when they're breaving heavy.'

Now the telephone rang. Leonard crossed to where it
stood on another smaller Swedish glass-and-steel table;
hesitated a moment before he picked up the receiver.
'Yes?' he said; and then his eyes flicked to the little band
of bent men occupying his chairs. He mouthed silently:
'It's him.'

It was him. The handsome man, in expectation of
whose arrival they were all gathered together in one
place. He should have brought report that the girl was
now putty under his hands, and maybe a key, or a good
impression of same, pressed into plasticine. He shouldn't
have been plastered all over a television screen, looking
like somebody bolted together by a mad scientist in a
bubbling cellar with no light save from the bunsen burner.

Leonard was speaking, in the lowered tone of vehement
anger that comes automatically to the telephone voice of
the bent at hint of trouble. 'What the hell you up to?'

Now he was listening.

Now he was speaking. 'I know. You stupid bastard.
You stupid bastard.'

The telephone talked to him again. He allowed it to do
so for a short time. Then he said, explosively: 'No. No.
Don't you come here. Sling it. But don't you come here,
mate—you're hot.'

CHAPTER 4

The Chinese restaurateur looked a bit askance when
Rosher, in company now with Detective-Sergeant Boggis,
knocked for the second time upon his door. Not merely

askance—perhaps not *even* askance, because dis-
concerted Chinese eyes can give that impression without
meaning to—but a little apprehensive. Say what you will,
in the most hospitable of countries the out-and-out alien
never rests quite easy, and if trouble is to come, he
expects that it will come from the police; who in his
country probably thrash about with batons and loose off
revolvers from all angles. It is well on the cards that he
thought he was about to be arrested for murder; which
would account for his eyes going glossy and his beam
spreading desperately wide as he sang:

'Hoo ha, Mlister Insplector. To whlat do I owe
honourh?'

'Bottles, Mr Wong,' said Rosher, who rarely used his
unctuous telephone-talk approach to anybody not female
unless the addressed was titled or hyphenated or possessed
of other powerful clout, and certainly never to China-
men. 'All yesterday's bottles.' Brusque tone, but not
overbearing.

'I have licence—' Mr Wong began, sure he was being
done for something. Should he offer a bribe? Thirty years
in this country, and he still never really knew what they
meant him to do at any problem moment. Inscrutable,
they were.

'We know you do, John.' This was Sergeant Boggis,
speaking out of turn again. Not to aggravate Rosher, but
simply because, like Rosher, he didn't care a monkey's if
he dealt aggravation or not. And Mr Wong's name was
not John. 'If you hadn't we'd have done you long ago. We
want all last night's bottles.'

'Hoo ha,' said Mr Wong. 'Hee hee hee.'

He led them to the kitchen, where last night's bottles
reposed higgledy-piggledy in a plaited raffia basket.
Nothing to raise a health inspector's eyebrows here.
Chinese wife and daughters presided, keeping everything
scrubbed and polished. 'Haven't washed 'em over, have

you?' Rosher asked.

Mr Wong was not sure whether yes or no would bring greater pleasure to two policemen so rugged and burly as to make him feel that he was made out of pipe-cleaners. To say no was, perhaps, to attract trouble directed to hygiene. To say yes might equally give rise to choler, for all he knew. He drew straws in his mind and said: 'No wash. Wash Monday.'

'Good, good,' said the man like a monkey in a black hat. 'What about the glasses?'

Mr Wong hedged his bet. 'All wash. Last night.'

'We'll take the lot, if it's all right with you.'

The sergeant spoke up again, grinning. 'We'll take the lot if it's not all right with you.'

'All light,' said Mr Wong, making little bows. 'All light, yes. You take, you take.'

They left him in the restaurant doorway, from which he turned away to a time of worry.

With the basket in the car boot, as Rosher let in the clutch the sergeant said: 'Ever hear the one about the Chinaman who couldn't pronounce his r's?'

'Yes,' said Rosher, very briefly.

'What, the Gleek Plick one?'

'Years and years ago.' And I don't want to hear it again from *any* bomb-headed oaf.

'Nothing much gets past you, does it?' said Sergeant Boggis.

There were lovely fingerprints on all the bottles, but they provided no positive clues. No way, since the lady at the table rarely handles the bottle, to tell which of these utterly unique finger-ends tipped wine into the glass of the girl around whose windpipe they later wrapped themselves. Rain and chill together obliterate prints, or even prevent their embossing, since they are formed by sweat; so the girl's body and its surroundings had yielded none to match with. But the fingerprint boys got to work, checking against the files, particularly those detailing sexual offenders. Nothing. Off went a man on a motor-cycle taking copies to the big city, while other copies went to London and all the forces up and down the country, sent by electrical impulse. They have this very handy little machine, called the Muirhead Transmitter.

By now it was afternoon, and settling to be a long, long day. Well, that's the way the business is. Hard on the feet, hard on the mind and no set duty pattern. Men on a major case often work seventy-two hours straight off, and another seventy-two after a couple of hours' kip on a truckle-bed in a makeshift murder room. More than that, if the job demands it. Wherefore, seasoned operators approach a case when they can without rush and pother, seeking to establish a rhythm that will stay them to the finish.

The Chief Constable was a seasoned man. So were Rosher and Boggis. So was Chief Superintendent (Percy) Fillimore; but Percy had a mind incapable of slow rhythms. A contented home life with plenty of sex might have unravelled him, but he wasn't very good at that sort of thing. So he fretted, from start of a case to finish; and if it never finished he took to himself a time of extra fret, believing in his secret heart that a man better at the job would have cleared it. He fidgeted now, the only one who did as the team sat in the comfortable chairs in the Chief's comfortable office, drinking tea and eating sandwiches (very good ones, well filled; they pull out fingers in police canteens when the Chief Constable orders), while waiting for the teleprinter to announce that somebody, somewhere, had record of some of those prints. Or not, as the case may be. Tea, sandwiches and discussion. Another innovation, this, that came when the Chief took over. Truth to tell, nobody enjoyed it much.

Rosher certainly didn't. Much as he owed this man,

there were times when he missed the more rugged days
when the old despot saw to it that East was East and West
was West and never the buggers mingled except at the
annual Policemen's Ball. Sitting here, he found half the
mind that should have been given to murder con-
centrated on not speaking with the mouth full, not
sucking tea through sandwich. Above all, not burping or
breaking wind; all of which things may be done freely in
the privacy of a man's home or office (provided he has no
pretty secretary, and Rosher had not) and commonly are
in police canteens. He sat and sipped with his little finger
sticking out, trying not to make small sibilances while the
Chief looked through the fingerprint blow-ups and all the
buff forms, photographs and assorted bumph accumu-
lating already around the case, saying:

'Not one of ours, then, it seems. Eh?'

The question was generally addressed. Percy, as chief
investigating officer, took it upon himself to reply. 'It
seems not, sir. No form, if he is. Our only sex offender
known to use violence is a man called Roebuck. Thomas
Roebuck. He's inside. Arnley, I believe.'

'Not an open prisoner?' Men have been known to walk
away from an open prison.

'No. Arnley.'

'Mm. Uh-huh.' The Chief tapped his teeth. They gave
out a little tocking sound, moving slightly. He frowned at
the post-mortem report. 'It seems she was not a virgin.'

Sergeant Boggis spoke from behind his sandwich. 'Who
is, nowadays?' He bit, and masticated like a bull.

'Mm. Mmm,' said the Chief. 'No close relatives—
orphanage turns out to be Bristol. Hm. Mm.' And as a
knock came on the door: 'Enter.'

It was a constable. Name of Purbright. Not that it
matters. 'Just in from the city, sir,' he said, handing over
the length of tape disgorged by the teleprinter.

'Thank you.' The Chief Constable received the tape.

Studied it as Constable Purbright left. Said: 'Unwieldly
way of doing things, one always thinks. Why don't they
just pick up the telephone? Ah. Ah-hah. What have we
here? Frederick Sidney Lugge. Alias Arnold
Trelawney—alias Cholmondely-Smythe—alias Vernon
Pemberton-Walker—alias—alias—alias— There we are,
Mr Fillimore. Over to you, I think.'

He passed the tape. Percy studied it. Under the sober
suiting his stomach went flip-flop and gave a small snarl.
He coughed to cover it. 'Interesting,' he murmured. 'Very
interesting.'

'I would suggest,' the Chief said, sitting back and
steepling his fingers, 'a quick call to the city. You can use
my phone. More tea, anybody?' Up here, tea came in a
pot with a concomitant jug of hot water. Nor was it drunk
out of thick clay mugs. 'No? To work, then, gentlemen,
shall we?'

Long before the town police had in hand his record of
malpractice, handsome Freddie Lugge, alias this and
alias that, who was not so handsome as he at first
appeared owing to craftiness about the eyes, received a
spectacular shock. In his flat in the big city he switched
on the radio for company's sake while he dressed and
made ready to visit that much better flat not far away
where Leonard Figgis lived. 'She can't be,' he said. 'Oh
Christ!'

What had happened was: into the sanctimonious mish-
mash buttered out by the BBC on a Sunday morning are
inserted news bulletins, perhaps to point up reproachfully
the undoubted fact that though they beaver away in the
vineyard week after week, year after year, nobody takes a
blind bit of notice. Freddie never even listened, he just
didn't like silence. But he heard this Upper Kensington
lady (or gentleman. Among BBC personnel the difference
is often minimal) announce the finding of a young girl's

body in Bishop Adam Park. They had the town named, they had the county; and to further shake him, they identified the girl and mentioned—mentioned? They laboured it, dragging in last year's attempted robbery; because anything to do with the old buzzard was news still—that she was maid to Sir Roland Goyt at his home, Nutley Towers. This was the only name they got wrong, which is not bad.

'She *can't* have been,' said Freddie aloud, all his dark hair brushed forward. From the mirror, chiselled lips and the eyes women—who, infatuated, never see craftiness—said were beautiful, both opened beyond norm, looked out at him with shock.

He settled his well-tended hair into its waves automatically and paced about the room for an hour, this being the length of time that separates news bulletins. He couldn't believe he'd heard it. He must hear it again. When he did, he went immediately forth to find a telephone. None in the flat. No television, either. One room he had in an anonymous apartment house. A base, that's all, for when he rested in this area, cheap to keep when he was away.

It was no longer early. The pubs were open. Freddie was not a man who parted from the blankets with the dew still on the day. He used the booth he normally used, set beside the Fiddler's Arms at the corner of the street; and as soon as the phone was lifted at the other end of the line he fumbled money into the slot and said: 'Leonard?'

'Yes?' said the phone, guardedly.

'It's Freddie.'

'What the hell you up to?' the phone demanded.

'Listen—she's dead. The bird—she's dead. Murdered.'

'I know. You stupid bastard,' said Leonard. 'You stupid bastard.'

Freddie's voice rose an octave. 'I didn't do it.' Clearly, the other man thought he had. 'I didn't do it, I swear it, she was all right when I left her. Listen—I got an impression. Plasticine.' She went to the lavatory, at the restaurant. Easy, in that secluded booth. She left her handbag and he seized the chance he'd known he could manufacture, if it didn't fortuitously come. Open the bag—out with the key—a quick press, and everything normal when she came back. 'I'm bringing it round—'

Leonard snapped in. 'No. No. Don't you come here. Sling it. But don't you come here, mate—you're hot.' And the phone went down, leaving Freddie with nothing for company but a buzz in the ear.

He found himself glancing furtively up and down the road before he emerged from the booth and walked the few yards to the Fiddler's Arms; where he ordered a whisky and stood at the bar, facing an implacable fact of life: there is no honour among thieves. Unless you have enormous financial resources—of which they will relieve you—or some sort of hold over them, when you fall into trouble your friends will melt away.

The Fiddler's Arms is one of those nasty pubs that fizz chemical beer out of metal taps and resound three nights a week to the neurotic cacophony of semi-professional groups called Blood, and The Wankers, and things like that. On Saturdays and Sunday evenings, these are joined by a fat, white compère who bellows dirty jokes. Needless to say, the place is very popular; and to sustain the ambience when no other din is happening, it possesses juke-boxes and machines that ping and ting and light up as the little ball goes round, and a bloated colour television flickering in desperate bid for attention from the corner of the light oak bar, all under lurid strip lighting.

It was this set, permanently on, that riveted Freddie when one o'clock came ten minutes after he arrived; and with it the news read by a lady successor to a lady who showed her legs on a comedy show and shot to instant stardom thereby. Nothing issuing from these dewy lips penetrated a screen of decibels from the juke-box, into which a lugubrious patron had just inserted silver and was receiving full value in exchange; but suddenly the lady vanished, to be replaced by pictures of policemen among trees; Detective-Sergeant Boggis emerging from trees; the Chief Constable mouthing against a background of trees; and finally, filling the whole screen, that coconut-tufted, slab-jawed degenerate.

Heart leaping, Freddie glanced covertly around the bar. Nobody was looking pointedly at him, or even at the television. A fair lunch-time crowd here; but all drinking, laughing, cupping ears, shouting at each other over the racket. *Why would they be looking at me?* he thought. *Thank Christ, I don't look like that.* Nevertheless, the butterflies beat in his belly. He finished his drink and went home, if you can call one crummy bed-sit in a crummy rooming house a home.

Here he stayed through an unpleasant hour or two; thinking: *I don't have to worry, I didn't do her in. Why should I? She was red-hot for it.*

Yes. But I've got form, haven't I? And the wireless reckoned she'd been raped.

The standard of intelligence among the small-time bent is not high, and Freddie was strictly small-time. Even so, nobody can buzz up against policemen from an early age without gathering a little pollen. So his mind ran on:

They'll track her back—they'll go to the bloody restaurant. They'll have been there by now—and the disco. Why have they put that picture out, plenty of people must have seen what I look like. I wasn't hiding.

Crafty. The bastards are crafty.

And anyway—the bottle. I handled the wine bottle. They'll go over everything like that, for dabs.

Then came the thought that stood his hair up, quivering.

Her handbag. Black plastic—perfect surface. My bloody dabs'll be all over it.

This was the clincher. The small-time bent, in time of dire extremity, by ratlike instinct scramble to go underground. His things—few but good; they all came as presents—shoved into his suitcase, Freddie crept down the stairs, tiptoed past the door behind which lurked the aged crone who lived there rent free in exchange for performing the washing, sweeping and spying duties that fall to the concierge in Paris, and went away rapidly, he knew not where, five minutes before two policemen arrived.

CHAPTER 5

The next morning, Chief Superintendent (Percy) Fillimore dropped out of the hunt. This is the way it happened.

He was in the Chief Constable's office, together with Inspector Rosher, Sergeant Boggis, Chief Superintendent (Uniform Branch) Rolly Rawlins and the Chief himself. Morning conference, and none of the men bleary because there was no pressing reason why they should not go to bed last night, ready to leap up at the tinkle of a phone. The Chief was studying a batch of new photographs issued already to the press and television people to replace that tufty-topped moron. This one showed Freddie Lugge, alias this, alias that, in film-idol three-quarter view, nicely lit to pick up the flash of teeth and indent of dimple. Not an official mug-shot—the city police, finding this on file along with the normal scowling full-front and profile, with commendable intelligence had

copied and sent it on as supplementary liable to be more
instantly recognizable, especially to women. The Chief,
then, was studying this picture and saying:

'What I do not understand is how we can have all those
people ringing in to say they'd seen the other fellow. The
Identikit fellow. I never do understand it, but it always
happens, doesn't it? No human ever looked like it, and yet
all those people know him or they've just seen him. Now
this one—yes. Yes—we ought to have a shoal of women
ringing in. Pity City missed him yesterday, but he
shouldn't prove too difficult.' Reasonable assumption. All
the morning papers carried the picture, this being a time
of flat in the news line. The name, too. In full, of course.
Frederick Sidney Lugge. Peculiarly ill-fitted to the
handsome face above; but then, John Wayne's real name
was Marion.

Inspector Rosher held in his hairy hands a copy of
Freddie's record. He said: 'Mm. Hmmm. Uh-huh. Nice
little feller.'

The Chief came up with a cliché. It is a privilege of
rank. 'Handsome is,' he said, 'as handsome does;' and one
of his pack of photos fluttered to the floor.

Now Percy was the officer standing closest. No longer
fretting, except about his stomach and the belief that he
was in for one of his nasty colds, seeded by standing about
in wet woods yesterday morning. The case, after all, was
open and shut. The man was missing, but an EMTAD was
out, his picture was to hand and plastered all over the
media. In the big city policemen were visiting all his
known haunts, looking up anybody believed to know him.
All over the country coppers were seeking him, leaving his
handsome likeness in hotels and boarding-houses—doing
all the things that would land him. Even if he contrived to
vanish utterly, and it can happen, no skin could be flayed
from Percy, he had done his part competently enough. So
now, without weight upon his mind beyond his normal

hypochondria, he bent as subordinates automatically do when top brass drops something, to retrieve the photo; and having bent remained so, clutching his back and saying: 'Oo—ergh—ooo!'

'What is it, Mr Fillimore?' the Chief asked.

'It's—oo—ooph—my back, sir,' Percy said. 'I—ooph—urgh—can't—oh oh—get up.'

Sergeant Boggis spoke. 'Slipped disc. The wife's uncle had one. We laid him down flat on the floor.'

What a blood silly thing to say. All very well behind one's own front door; but a Detective-Superintendent, lying flat on his back in a Chief Constable's office? Unthinkable. And for how long, even if the Chief Constable, as a humane man, invites it? For how long, with people lifting the leg to step over as the busy workaday goes by? Ridiculous.

The Chief said: 'Oh dear. How unfortunate. I've heard that sometimes when you straighten up they click back in again.'

'I—can't—straighten up, sir,' said Percy, standing there like a very ham amateur actor playing Third Witch in *Macbeth*. 'It seems to have—oo—oo!'

'Oh dear, oh dear,' the Chief said. 'Will you be able to—that is—er—should we, do you think, fetch the doctor in?'

'I'll—be all right, sir,' said Percy. 'I think perhaps I'd better—oo—ah.'

Now the Chief spoke crisply. One of the qualities that lifts a man to high rank is the ability to make crisp and clean decision, right or wrong. 'Hospital. Get it looked at.'

In his heart, Percy was with him every inch of the way. That sensitive hypochondria leaped about like a goldfish into whose bowl has slipped a sudden piranha. He would never get up again, he was crippled forever, his only view of the world from now on a few square yards of whatever terrain he was tottering over, and his feet. But he made the effort. Whatever is said about policemen, and many people say many things, they are hard men to down. 'I'm—all right really, sir. It's just—my back.'

'Mr Rosher,' said the Chief, 'perhaps you will support Mr Fillimore on one side, and you, Sergeant, on the other. I shall ring down for the ambulance. It should be at the door by the time you get there.' Obviously, they were not going to gallop.

So exit Percy to St Barnolph's Hospital, in the police ambulance with light flashing and siren shrieking; not because there was desperate emergency, but because if you are two young constables suddenly lumbered with a Chief Superintendent in obvious agony, you want him to know that you are doing everything within your power to speed him to succour.

Detective-Inspector Rosher remounted the stairs beside Sergeant Boggis, his shoulders not bowed by grief. On the contrary, he found it difficult to prevent the chuckle vibrating in his belly from spreading to the corners of his mouth. Sergeant Boggis said: 'Bloody painful, that is, you know. The wife's uncle wears a corset.'

'Uh-huh,' said Inspector Rosher. Nothing surprises a policeman. He'd known men who wore frilly knickers.

The Chief, when they re-entered, was alone. Chief Superintendent Rolly Rawlins, who played walk-on throughout and who attended these meetings anyway only because protocol demanded it—uniform branch activity in a murder case is all routine, bound by prescribed regulations—was gone. The Chief sat at his solid mahogany desk playing with the little pistol that was really a lighter, used to kindle cigarettes before he gave up smoking.

He said: 'Ah—gentlemen. Here's a pickle.'

'Mm,' said Inspector Rosher.

'Very painful condition, sir,' said Sergeant Boggis.

'Oh, indeed, indeed. No doubt about that. But, of course, it leaves us without a head. Most unfortunate.'

'Uh-huh,' said Inspector Rosher.

'Superintendent Pritikin is still on leave. Marrakesh, I believe; one would be very reluctant to call him back. After all, the case seems straightforward enough. You can handle it, Mr Rosher, I take it? Under my jurisdiction, of course.'

The chuckle in the belly of Inspector Rosher was joined by a small singing bird. Percy off his back and laid low to boot. On his own again—and it was all his. Because direction from the Chief must perforce be nominal. A chief constable has many, many cases, all happening simultaneously under his jurisdiction.

All right: so there was nothing to be done at this moment; and when the running man was apprehended, not much more than to collect him from whatever force held him, fetch him back here and tidy the loose ends. Never mind—what the Chief was saying was: Alfred, it's all yours. 'No problem, sir,' said Alfred Stanley Rosher.

'Good. Good. Keep me informed.' The Chief switched his eyes to his in-tray and stretched a white-cuffed hand to fasten on the bumph next to be dealt with. His henchmen tramped away; not to strenuous endeavour in the prosecution of this case, but to take up again until it cracked their normal routine poking into the smaller manifestations of mankind's naughty side, interrupted by the call of murder.

Frederick Sidney Lugge was gone beyond them. All they could do for now was wait. Detective-Inspector Rosher's boxy-toed, lace-up shoes went lightsome down the stairs. To him now would come all the phone-calls from people who knew Frederick Sidney, or thought they did; or had just seen him. Or thought they had. Press interest, too, would be funnelled to him, and his would be the name appearing in the papers, on radio, on television. Reason enough for a lightsome step. Publicity, unless it refers to corruption or bungling, is as welcome to a policeman as to any man who relies for his living on a public image.

'You're the boss, then, eh?' said Sergeant Boggis, as they clacked along the corridor that resounded less beneath the heavy tread since they put compo flooring down.

'Uh-huh,' went Rosher, turning aside to his office; while his mind said: And don't you bloody well forget it, cock.

There is no point in mincing words. Freddie Lugge was neither a strong man nor an intelligent one. But he was a man in a sticky situation. For one thing, he had very little money on him. Train fares alone, and this brooks no argument nowadays, swathe through what is left after a man who thought he'd be calling at the bank on Monday has invested in a Chinese meal with wine, not even going dutch with the girl on a Saturday night. And he left by train, his car being locked away in a big city garage, having a little welding done to expedite its MoT certificate. There's the trouble with the British Sunday, quite apart from its unholy boredom. Everything locked away until Monday. Including your money, if you do not keep it in a sock.

Not many people in the England of today travel by train on any day, and fewer still on Sunday. The British are not all idiots, and few are stinking rich. So Freddie had a carriage to himself all the way to King's Cross, which afforded decent privacy for the thumbing over of his money; and he found—the discovery added to his stress—that he hadn't enough left even for a night in one of those ill-natured little boarding-houses that stud the grubby streets around the London termini. A dweller in rented accommodation, quite often travelling to vanish,

though never before without pre-planning, he knew the
cost of it. And that's just for a bed, with a cup of instant
coffee and a snippet of stale dough shaped like a croissant
in the morning, styled Continental Breakfast by the
proprietor or trix. Whichever the sex, it should walk
about with a knife between its teeth.

Now further abroad in London, in the Brixtons and
the Claphams, in Shoreditch and Stepney and Hackney
Wick and all around Kennington Oval way, accommodation may be had at a less villainous rate; but
between you and it, if you start from any terminus, stands
the even greater villainy of London Transport. So small a
sum remained with Freddie that he feared arriving in one
of these less rapacious districts still unable to afford the
night's lodging, having been forced to feed those evil little
machines at the top of Underground escalators.

If this happened, a man in a good suit wandering all
night with a pigskin suitcase would attract more
attention, particularly from the police and marauding
gangs of thuggish persuasion, than the same man in the
less personalized purlieus of a big station, where men in
good suits with cases are commonplace at night because
they tend to miss the last train or are here for a late one.
They shelter, many of them, in waiting-rooms, along with
the regular night inhabitants: the winoes and junkies and
dead-beats and so on; and the refugees from fights with
the wife and things of that order. Faceless and
anonymous, these men, collar-huddled and kipping or
brooding silent upon the evil day that married them.

So Freddie did what was, in the circumstances, the
sensible thing. He hung around as though waiting for a
train, easily evading on busy platforms the couple of
wandering policemen who came by. He lingered at a
corner table in the buffet over plastic pie and chips until
darkness came down; when he found himself a seat on a
hard waiting-room bench. He spent the night here,

unsleeping except for a doze towards dawn; on one side a wooden arm-rest where the bench ended, and on the other a scabrous tramp in a filthy old raincoat, sagged against him and snoring uproariously. More people snore, and grind their teeth, and mutter in their sleep than is generally realized by those who never spent a night in a railway waiting-room.

Big shock came in the morning. Stiff and chilled, he stayed hunched on that bench in spite of aching until the room began to empty; because for long after dawn paled the lamps and showed up stubble and bleariness all around, the station outside remained deserted. A man going out there would be very noticeable, echoing over the concrete. Eventually, though, the outgoings from here meant that the men remaining would be almost as personalized. By this time early workers were arriving on the platforms, hawking and grumbling and waiting for short-distance trains. Soon the station would be well peopled with commuters coming in. He picked up his suitcase and ventured forth.

It was very chilly. Through the night-crumpled light coat and scruffy-feeling suit the spring nip shivered his too long unfed body. He found the public lavatory and descended to do what universal mankind must do, first thing in the morning. A mirror above a washbasin showed him white and stubbled, dark shadows already under the beautiful but crafty eyes. All he did about it was comb his hair. He would wash and shave later, when other basins were tenanted. Not down here all alone.

He rose to the surface. Not far away a gummy-eyed news-stand assistant rolled upward a clattering metal blind. It revealed a second assistant standing within the booth, cutting securing string from bundles of newspapers and laying a pack of each overlapping along the counter.

Freddie hesitated. He needed a paper, he needed to

know what was happening. Not in the great big world, to hell with oil crises and Middle East wars and Ronald Reagan and Maggie Thatcher and all the other ills mankind was currently inflicting upon itself; but with regard to his own matter: whether they were on to him, and if so did they know where he'd gone, or even that he was gone. But: between him and aquisition of a paper loomed fear. He hovered awhile, arguing with it; saying to himself:

You're panicking. Don't be bloody stupid. Who's going to recognize you? You're nothing like that Identikit picture. Anyway—look—look—see that feller? He just grabbed a paper, shoved his money over, and the geezer in the booth didn't even look up, he's got his mind on sorting the gear out. And the bloke who shoved the shutter up's got his head under the counter now, sorting stuff out with his back towards you. Go on—get in now. Sod it—you don't even know they know it was you she was with on Saturday. Look—there goes another geezer— shoves his money over and grabs a paper. Gone, rushing for his train. Get in, quick. Maybe you can go home, maybe they've nicked somebody. You've been belting about in a panic—maybe you needn't have come at all. Maybe you can contact somebody up here— Iris—she's crazy about you—she'll let you have the money for the fare home.

He shifted the case in his hand—it was getting very heavy—and moved towards the booth. Now came the big, tingling shock.

From the top tabloid page his unmistakable face smiled out at him. Where'd they get that picture? It wasn't a mug shot, it was one he'd had taken when he was trying to break into the movies. Some crafty bastard of a copper must have half-inched it, last time he got done.

He hurried on past the booth, and in new panic out from the station. Even with nowhere to go, shock the man already scared and running, and he ups with his skirt and travels very nimbly, away from the point of concussion.

Leonard Figgis, now—he was a man of different weight entirely. No more intelligent than Freddie, and certainly not his match for imagination; but for sheer, dogged tenacity nobody could fault him. He was rough and he was tough; and whereas prison in all-male company crippled Freddie, who attracted considerable attention from men deprived and sick of lonely masturbation, Leonard took porridge when he had to without stress. It is, after all, integral to the bent way of life.

If reason deeper than natural cowardice is needed to explain Freddie's premature panic, consider the fact that many of these characters resort to rape. It had happened to Freddie more than once since his first incarceration as a rosy boy, when he served as material for a gang-bang, five inmates and a bent screw. Bad nick, that was, the governor himself went in soon after. Leonard never panicked in his life; but then, who'd want to rape Leonard? Apart from being rough and tough, he was big and ugly.

Very likely it was due entirely to this difference in man-appeal that while Freddie was skulking in the streets of London later that morning, Leonard walked up and down the thick carpet of what was really a luxury apart-ment—the bent do not have to be super-successful to become relatively rich; in the purely material sense, crime is one business that does pay, given nerve and proper organizing—and that to one of the henchmen seated in one of his Swedish chairs who had asked a question he was saying, not without vehemence:

' 'Course I know it's there. Ernie Parvis said so. Right, Horsehead?'

James (Horsehead) Rumblelow, ugly as his leader and bigger, and so much dimmer, said: 'Yeah. You firken know he did, dontcher? You all firken know he did.'

'I didn't say he didn't,' said Charlie Palkin. 'What I said was: how do we know Ernie wasn't bumming his chat? You know—geezers often do, don't they, in stir?'

The man Parvis, ex-secretary to Sir Roland Goyt, would be inside for a long time. But in for a good deal longer was Mr Henry Croker, who organized the ill-fated raid and whose Judas-man he was. Bumming his chat, incidentally, means bragging. People do it often inside prisons.

'He told Horsehead because Horsehead was coming out. Right? So he could pass the word on so there'd be a little something stashed for him when *he* comes out. Right?' Leonard, this was.

'We was sharing this cell,' said Horsehead, 'and he says to me—'

'I know what he said.' Charlie waved him down. 'You told us. That's why we're all here, ain't it? Question is—*if* he ain't bumming—what do we do about it? I mean—you know. Glamour-boy's buggered it, ain't he?'

'Not necessarily.' Leonard was not the man to give up potential big tickle so easily. Tenacity. Out of it and a certain fertility in planning came the wall-to-wall carpet, the expensive appurtenances, leadership of this happy band and all. Mind you, the British gang system is not so tightly knit as in the America of Al Capone, or even the Mafia. People drift in and out. But they always came when he called. 'Not necessarily. Who else works there?'

'Where?' asked Bernie Stephens.

'The house, you twat. Who else works in it?'

'Well—I don't know, do I?'

'How do we know?' Charlie said. 'Never been near it, have we?'

'Well, then,' said Leonard, 'we'd better find out.'

'You can't go near the house,' Bernie said.

'Why not?'

'Well—the Old Bill'll be watching it, won't they?'

'Why? The bird wasn't done there, was she? She just happened to be the maid, he done her in the park. Sex murder, ain't it? They won't be watching for him around the house, will they? He never even went there, not such a prat as that, was he? Met her in the town. Well, then.'

The brightest face among his henchmen, and this was Charlie's, took on a thoughtful look. 'Yeah. I see what you mean.'

'I don't,' said Horsehead. He never did. He was here only because he was the one into whose big, thick cauliflower Parvis whispered secrets, to be passed on to Leonard.

'Christ!' Leonard said. 'Listen—she wasn't the only staff. Right? Big house like that? So who else is there? Who's bent? Anybody? Who's got keys, who knows the security system? You was going in, Charlie, right, when he'd got the key?'

'Yeah.' That had been the plan. Charlie in beforehand, to make a hole in that system. He could do it all right, nobody better. Earned a good living at it. A wire here reattached there—a beam ruptured—the owner would never even know about it until the boys were in and gone. Very clever fingers. Self-taught, too, never went to college or anything. Well, neither had Bernie, and look at him. One of the best safe-crackers in the business, that's all.

'So maybe,' Leonard said, 'there's somebody who'll let you in. Or something. Worth a look, annit?'

'Come to think about it,' said Charlie, 'you could be right, at that.'

'Drive over there now, then, eh? Just to hang your eyeballs out.'

CHAPTER 6

On the following morning, after another good night's sleep, Detective-Inspector Rosher set out with Detective-Sergeant Boggis for London, to pick up Frederick Sidney Lugge, whom they believed could assist them with their enquiries; by which time, Charlie had reported back to Leonard in the big city that it looked as though the only staff left in the vicinity of Sir Roland Goyt were a cook-housekeeper living in and a gardener who occupied a cottage in the grounds. Before even the chickens were up, a dark blue car left the town police station driven by Sergeant Boggis.

A good time for driving, with no impeding traffic on the roads, and the countryside looking very beautiful as the sky lightens and flushes when the sun comes up on a bright spring morning; but Rosher had no love for the country, not even for this exceptionally blessed six-mile segment of hills and fecund valleys, of rivers and fields dotted with mellow farms and villages enobling the road from the town until it connects with the motorway. Nor was he a morning talker, preferring until he was dug well into the day a decently morose reticence. Unfortunately, Sergeant Boggis was a talker. Some are, some are not.

Right from the start, he talked. And said nothing, really. Nothing of interest or import. Your morning talker does not need pithy subject-matter, all he needs is to talk until the interior gears mesh to the day's proper rhythm. And to whistle through the pauses. A matter of body chemistry, or something. It raises the hackles of those not similarly cursed, even when it burbles from a loved one; and Rosher's soul took no delight in Sergeant Boggis. So thirty miles along the motorway, as they bombed towards London, he stirred in his hunched corner and snarled:

'For Christ's sake knock it off, will you?'

'Knock what off?' said Sergeant Boggis, surprised.

'The bloody nattering. You've been at it ever since we set out.'

'Who has?' A rising of indignation, to mingle with the surprise. Sufferers rarely know they are doing it, and are apt to take umbrage when it is pointed out to them.

'You have. All the bloody way.'

'Well—get you, mate.' Two sets of hackles in the car, bristling on almost identical napes.

Rosher blared, immediately. 'And we'll have a little respect, son, while we're at it.'

Things trembled on the sergeant's tongue; but he fought them down, knuckles whitening on the wheel. From now on, through town and country and all the urban mess of commuter-complex and suburb that lie between here and Islington he drove in seething silence, his mind constructing variations on the theme: Respect? For you, you old twat? I should bloody cocoa.

Freddie collected, the return journey was accomplished in equally fraught silence; which frightened him, sitting handcuffed in the back after a night alone with his imagination in a cell. Not that your experienced policeman ever does much in the way of talking when he conducts a newly arrested body from point to point. Silence after a night of cell-silence is a well-proven ploy, it often starts the subject babbling. But this silence had an added quality, translated in Freddie's imagination as malevolence directed towards him.

Poor Freddie. Some are born inept. He was picked up in the early evening by the London police, who did not realize then what they had copped. By the time they did, and passed the news on, it was getting late. 'Fetch him in the morning,' the Chief Constable said. 'No point in driving all that way and back now, it will take half the night. Get away early in the morning.'

This was sensible. Freddie was secured, and tomorrow might see long, long hours of interrogation, everybody cooped in an increasingly stale interview room. Start fresh, whenever you can. No joy in running yourself ragged. Let him stew for a night, in a cell. Just for starters.

Inevitable, of course, that he would be tapped on the shoulder in the end; but what he did to bring it about so expeditiously was as silly as had been his scarpering in the first place.

From King's Cross he went via Grays Inn Road to Holborn. That way and to the west he knew well enough, but not the dreadful hinterland to the east and the waste of wide highways going nor'west by north. Panic instinctively clings to the familiar; so off he went up Grays Inn Road, and by the time he got to Holborn the rush hour was under way.

Well, now: he was running scared, but not so scared that it blanked out his mind entirely. He knew that crowd is cover. A man viewed in isolation is a man. In a London crowd, viewed by the crowd, he is faceless; or if not that, the impact of any one face is dulled in minds distracted with the cattle-crushing problem of getting from point here to point there in the rush hour, even if that face has just been eyed in newsprint. No aid to concentration, hanging from a tube-train strap or sitting squashed up against a lady who might, with benefit to the community, bathe more often. So he mingled, walking west. Up, for those who know the area, to the New Oxford Street end.

No problems. All those faces went rushing by, thyroid-eyed, white, showing symptoms of high communal stress; and nobody glanced at him twice. Apart, that is, from the odd woman still capable in the morning of sexual involvement. A woman or two always did look at Freddie, as did a man or two. But those who looked now rushed on, lest they enrage Big Brother by a tardy start to the day's servility. So his mingling worked.

But it did not ease his basic situation. His own face was white—and, what was worse, showing dark stubble. Stubble and dungarees—yes. Stubble and a dapper, spring-catalogue coat, a good suit, a fine suitcase wrought from the skin or skins of a pig or pigs—no. A drizzle began.

There is, up towards the west end of Holborn, a public pissoir set under an island in the middle of the road. Generations of men have descended into it, found ease, come out and died. Not immediately, it's not that bad; but eventually. Dammit, it's been there through two world wars, it dates back to the day of the hansom cab. Down into this haven went Freddie; and feeling it safer here than at the station, unzipped his case and whipped out his battery razor. In less than two minutes he was reasonably smoothed and up again, making progress against the human current flowing out from Holborn tube station; until past the station entrance, he was borne along by that part of it washing into New Oxford Street.

The London rush hour lasts until about 9.30. He walked in it until then, relatively safe, moving at the pace of it all along Oxford Street, down Regent Street to Piccadilly Circus, through Leicester Square to Charing Cross Road—by this time the crowd was thinning—and so back to the beginning of Oxford Street. About to embark again on the same journey, tiring already because a case is very heavy, lugged along forever, he paused and turned aside, back towards Holborn. There are police always in Oxford Street, and they watch for men with cases. These men arrive, glance around, open up their cases and begin to flog. Cheap perfumes, toys, monster balloons, anything sufficiently portable fallen from the back of a truck. At the approach of police, up with the case and scarper. He who is slow off the mark gets nicked. It's a harmless diversion, enjoyed particularly by the police. Breaks up the monotony of the daily grind.

An idea came, as he neared Holborn station. That pissoir. There'd been no attendant. Would there be one now? Down under could be sanctuary, and privacy while he thought things out.

As a matter of interest: the attendant normally incumbent, a Mr Bert Harker who lived hard by the Elephant and Castle, failed to report for duty today, laid low with a dose of shingles; so Freddie was able to insert his paltry fee and sit unmolested all the way up through the morning; private, but suffering ever more acutely from hunger.

At one o'clock he took another chance. The lunch-time rush for snackbar sandwiches would be on now. He crept forth; joined a queue; bought two of ham and two of cheese; returned unchallenged to his bolt-hole and consumed them. Felt better. Thought again what he had thought before:

Iris. She's the only one.

But Iris lived in Islington. A long way to walk; but he could get a bus, just up the road from here. She wouldn't be at her flat, she'd be at work. So? He knew where she kept the spare key.

Go there, he said to himself. You can't sit here forever. She'll see you right—you can handle her. Crazy about you.

What the fool should have done, of course, was hand himself in at the nearest police station. Say he understood they wanted to see him, he came up to London on business, reported in as soon as he learned his presence was desired. Instead, he caught that bus to Islington. Very edgy ride; but a man is less exposed to public scrutiny on a bus, once he's weathered the conductor, than he is plodding along through Clerkenwell to the

Angel with a pigskin suitcase.

There is a small area in Islington given over to little antique shops and chi-chi bric-à-brac. This is where Iris lived, behind the only door in a small alley. When you were in you went upstairs, and were above one of these shops. The key was where she always kept it—in a small niche where cement was missing between two bricks above the door, hidden from ground level by a rain-porch. The things people do.

Nothing had changed inside, except that the bed now had a brown overlay where it used to have blue. Nothing much does change, in flats rented furnished. There were eggs in the fridge. He ate them as an omelette, with bread and butter, washing them down with tea. Iris wouldn't grudge it.

No liquor about. Pity—if ever he needed a drink! And rest. He'd lie on the bed, shoes off at last, and wait.

Oh, thank God. Thank God. Out of sight. Snug, lying on the bed wherein so often . . . But not for some months. Hadn't passed this way.

Iris wouldn't let him down. She adored him. A kiss or two, a flutter of the tongue, a stroking with the hands . . . She wouldn't let him down.

Please God she wouldn't. But—and who knew better than he?—women are kittle cattle. Well—he'd no option, nowhere else to go. He needed money from her, at least. He'd have to back his skill. And in this, at least, he could trust.

When Miss Charmian fford-Lewis, unmarried teetotal primary school teacher of retiring habit and indefinite age, came into the flat yielded up two weeks ago by her predecessor Miss Iris Golightly, she was surprised to find all her eggs eaten up, shells on the draining-board, bread and butter together with dirty crockery on the kitchen table. 'Somebody's been in,' she whispered. 'Perhaps he's still here.'

It had to be a man. Men brought the violence, the terror into life. And a woman, if she hadn't washed up, at least would have put the shells in the tip-top garbage can.

She crept into the living-room. There stood a pigskin case, obviously to hold her personal treasures after he had raped and killed her. Heart standing still—she swears to this day that it stood still—expecting at any moment the locking of hairy hands about her cold-sweating throat, she crept back through the kitchen, along the short passage—it creaked! It creaked!—and out from the front door. The Yale lock secured itself softly behind her. She rushed now from the alley to the little shop beside it, crying hysterically: 'Mr Pimm—Mr Pimm—there's a man in my flat!'

Directly above, utterly exhausted, Freddie Lugge slept on. Even the policemanly hand on his shoulder failed to arouse him at first. It fell at about the time when Charlie Palkin, on behalf of friends and associates, made first contact with Oliver Hardcastle, handyman-gardener to Sir Roland Goyt.

Now, on this bright and sunny morning, he came back into the town in a plain blue car, with a coat thrown over his head to foil a clutch of press photographers, and flanked by two grimly silent and burly men who seemed to have no objection to their own pictures being taken. They handed him over to an equally hostile-looking uniform sergeant, and tramped in silence away.

All very frightening. He was a-gibber when Rosher and Boggis returned to the interview room where the uniform sergeant decanted and left him to further silence, with a guard on the door, while they spoke to the Press before ingesting plastic-wrapped pie (Mr Cracknel's Noted Pork) and mahogany tea in the upstairs canteen. 'Listen,' he said as they came in, 'I didn't do her.'

Reply came from the one even more like a gorilla out of

his black hat than in it. 'You told the Islington police you didn't even know her.'

'They—rattled me.' This, undoubtedly, was the truth. Waking under a heavy hand, that hand attached to a policeman, is to the guilty a deeply rattling experience. Instinctive reaction is to deny all knowledge of whatever malodorous matter brought the copper here. They all do it. It's expected of them.

'So now you know her.' The gorilla man, a folder in his hairy hands, crossed the bare, stark room, approaching with intent to be seated a hard chair behind a hard desk, before which, on another hard chair, they had put Freddie. No other furniture in the room and only one little window, very high up. Walls in evil olive-green below waist level, dull ochre above. Interview rooms are designed with hostility in mind. They are a weapon. The other hard man leaned himself against one of those uncharitable walls, silently bringing out a nail file.

'I didn't do her.'

'We have reason to believe otherwise.' Inspector Rosher had gained the chair and seated himself upon it. He opened the folder.

'I didn't—'

'One moment, my son. One moment.' Little hard eyes were studying paper. They had passed over it before, but not to reveal the fact is theatrically effective. 'Mm. Mm. Uh-huh. Nice little feller, aren't you? Quite the specialist. Lonely ladies, eh? Pick up their savings with one hand while you tickle 'em up with the other. Nice line in aliases, too. Roger Courtenay-Williams. Alistair Trevillion. How do you like that, Sergeant?'

'Nice,' the leaning man said, exploring for dirt with his file. 'Very nice. Touch of class.' Stupid old twat, his mind was saying still.

'That was for a Miss Travers-Poultenoy, at Maidenhead. They like a bit of class in Maidenhead.' The folder,

the papers were laid aside. 'All right, son—you know your
rights. You don't have to answer questions, but it looks
very bad if you don't, the way I tell the beak when you
appear in court.'

'I didn't do her,' said Freddie.

'We have semen samples. And the gear in your case is
in the lab now.'

'All right—so I had sex with her. But I didn't do her.'

'In my day,' the sergeant said, quite unsolicited, 'the
two things were synonymous.'

The inspector barked. 'Thank you, Sergeant.' Visibly,
handsome Freddie jumped. Those mean little eyes came
back to him. 'Better tell us about it, son. I shall be very
hard on you if you don't.'

So Freddie spoke. He told it as it was; except that he
left out any mention of Leonard, or of any ulterior motive
behind his taking the girl out and cocking a leg over her
where bushes form a screening alcove, down by the edge
of the lake. Which lake had been well dragged by now, in
a search for the girl's handbag.

'So,' said the inspector when he had finished, 'what
made you scarper?'

'I knew you'd—I thought you'd—'

'You knew we'd know you'd done her,' said the
sergeant; and got himself, this time, hissingly glared at.
Oh, hard, hard bastards, these two were. Didn't even like
each other.

'I didn't do her,' Freddie said. On a note of desperation
now.

'Let's put it like this,' the gorilla man said. 'You take
this plain little girl out, you spend quite a little bundle on
feeding her, we've got a copy of the bill. You come all the
way from the city, to do that and then to stuff—to have
intercourse with her under a bush by the lake. Why?'

'I—liked her. She was a nice girl.'

'You liked her. And yet when you finished you left her

there, just like that, to find her own way home.'

'I—it wasn't far. There was a bus—I told you, I had to
get the train, my car's out of action.' I truly did.

'Never going to call you Gentleman Freddie Lugge, are
they, Alistair? So off you scarper to London, and wind up
with a bit of burglary.'

'That was a mistake—I got in with a key—a bird I
knew lived there—.'

Actually, even the Islington police and Miss Charmian
fford-Lewis had accepted this story, although the woman
Iris had not yet been traced. Why should they not? Any
other was too ludicrous. Freddie would be charged, if
anybody bothered—and they wouldn't, in view of the big
charge he had to face—only with trespass. But when you
pile, pile on thick. It all helps.

'What did you do with her handbag?' the inspector
asked.

'Handbag?'

'You know what a handbag is. We've got a description
here. Black plastic. Plated metal clasp, gold colour.'

'I never touched her handbag.'

'Let's start again, at the top. You met her on Saturday
evening. Right? At the bus station. Why?'

'I liked her.'

'I hope you're sitting comfortably, son. We could be in
for a long session . . .'

At approximately the time when they sat Freddie down
on that hard little chair, Charlie Palkin entered a
telephone kiosk and dialled Leonard Figgis's number.

When the party at the other end answered, and he had
asked if it was Leonard, and the party admitted
guardedly that it was, Charlie said: 'Listen—I've just had
a good shufti at this gardener geezer. He's Ollie
Hardcastle.'

'Who's Ollie Hardcastle?'

'Strangeways. I was with him in Strangeways.'

'That's handy. Old mate, is he?'

'Well—no. Not really. He hadn't got no mates, he was in for mucking about with little girls. We was three to a cell. Some of the boys beat him up, that's really how I remember the name. Disciplinary enquiry. I mean—I didn't mix with him, or nothing like that.' Child molesters lead a grim and lonely life in prisons.

'Pity. Pity he's not one of the boys. You know they've got Lugge, don't you? Just heard it on the wireless.'

'No. Have they? I've been in a shed. On the edge of the garden. Sod it.

'Well—it may not be him. Said a man's helping 'em with their enquiries.'

'Yeah—well, it would. What do you reckon, then?'

'You sure this geezer's this Hardacre geezer?'

'Hardcastle. Yeah—I got a good look at him, he's mowing the lawn. 'Course, he's grown a beard. And his hair's long. That's why I didn't get him straight away.'

'And you reckon he's bent?'

'Well—got to be, ain't he? If he ain't, I can help him along a bit. Not much bother.'

Two minds in close accord, both well aware that the other was beavering along in the same direction. Both wool-dyed villains, waiting a long time for tickle as big as this. Once in a lifetime such opportunity knocks. Think of the crown upon a career, think of what you can buy with all that loot. Think—oh, think. Think of the wine, the women. And the song, if you incline that way.

'Reckon it could be our lucky day,' said Leonard.

'So long as our boy ain't spieling.'

'He won't. Know why? His pretty kisser's his stock in trade, ain't it? He knows he ain't going to have it long, if he don't keep his trap shut.'

'Suppose they find the key pattern on him?'

'If he's got any sense it's down a drainhole somewhere.'

As a matter of fact, it was flushed down that Holborn lavatory. 'Listen—how does it look your end?'

'Quiet. No Old Bill about.'

'Good. There won't be, no reason why they'd come up there. Can you fade, if they do?'

'No problem,' Charlie said. 'There's this shed, woods behind it right down to the road. Plenty of cover.'

'Well—don't take no chances, if they roll up get clear. We'll hang it up for a while. But if you think it's okay, see what you can do with this Hardapple geezer.'

'Hardcastle. You reckon we ought to go ahead, then?'

'Don't want to lose it, do we? And he couid be just what we needed.'

Again the empathy. No need for either little voice to tell the other what it already knew: that if Ernie Parvis whispered to Horsehead, and nothing happened, he might well whisper to somebody else. A lot of people bigger than Leonard would be very, very interested. Many besides Charlie would consider it a doddle.

'Yeah. Right,' said Charlie. 'I'll get on to it. If you want me in a hurry, I'm booked in at the Unicorn. I'll ring you when I've tapped into this geezer.'

'Whaddaya say his name is?'

'Ollie Hardcastle. Dirty bastard.'

Charlie hung up and went back to his car. He re-entered that handy shed with a loose board in the back at precisely the time when Detective-Inspector Rosher and Detective-Sergeant Boggis washed down the crumbs of their pork pies with the dregs of the teak-brown tea and rose to go back to the interview room. The gardener was working still, riding his mower up and down the lawn. It made a good, green smell.

He was Ollie Hardcastle, all right. Charlie settled down, to wait. No good rushing things. Foolish, to make overtures that might meet hostility under the eyes of the house. Make sure Freddie Lugge's arrest had sparked off no fuzz interest, tap softly on the cottage door when this geezer had knocked off and was settling to a nice kipper. Veteran of many a casing, all through the time when Freddie was being insulted and barked at, coaxed and flattered, he kept himself comfortable with sandwiches from the small soft bag brought with him, and a little fruit to balance the diet. He even had a vacuum flask filled with hot coffee, and when he needed a wee-wee he did it in a corner of the hut. Not very nice for the spider who had lived there this many years, completely undisturbed.

He quite expected that the man, who wore a beard now, and longer hair than meets favour in Strangeways, would come to the shed at some time during the afternoon, perhaps to collect shears or something, or to park the mower; and this would have suited him nicely. Nobody to witness their meeting; the advantage of shock maximized; and time for Ollie to gather himself together before he went out again. But he didn't come, he mowed a while and left the mower standing while he clipped a few roses and dug a bit and planted something out for summer. A gardener's work is never done.

At half past five he drove the mower across and Charlie moved to stand facing the door; but still the man did not come in. He left the machine beside the shed, covering it with a tarpaulin; and went, not right-handed towards the main gate, but left-handed across the lawn and out from a side gate into the lane from which Charlie crept through trees and shrubbery to where he was now, in the shed.

Charlie moved swiftly, squeezing himself through the loose back-boarding. The geezer could turn either way, left or right. It didn't matter which, the lane was private, sunk between bushes and deserted.

Ollie turned left; which brought him to where Charlie popped out from a bush right beside him, saying cheerfully: 'Hallo, Ollie.'

The gardener stopped dead, almost staggered back; because he had been expecting, all keyed up with fear, that somebody would appear out of the blue to say something like this at any moment, and to cart him away. As well he might, since this was the man who murdered the girl. He said: 'Who—who—who are you?' Charlie's actuality had not yet superimposed itself over the copper-image fear-stamped on his inner eye.

'You remember me,' said Charlie, all smiles. 'Charlie Palkin, we was in Strangeways together. You all right? You've gone a very funny colour.'

'Stra—Stra—I wasn't in Strangeways,' said Ollie.

Charlie's smile grew wider, more friendly yet. 'Oh, yes, you was. Nothing to be ashamed of, it happens to us all some time or other.'

'I—I don't know you.' But he did, and a man as sharp as Charlie Palkin could see it in his eyes. Could see it in all the grey face visible under a thick beard holed now by the shocked and trembling mouth.

'Yes, you do,' said Charlie, encouragingly. 'And if you don't, it don't matter, because you will very soon. Where you off to?'

'A per—a per—a per—a pint,' Ollie said. Answering truthfully, too shocked to know what he was doing. He always went for a pint after work, at a pub down the road called the Green Man. Nice little pub, all thatched and oak-beamed.

'Good—I'm going to buy you one, for old time's sake. In the town, though, not here. My car's just down the road. Come on, me old china. How's life been treating you since you got out?' Charlie took hold of a quivering arm to lead the man away; and Ollie, knowing him as that Charlie Palkin who, when it came to the time for beating up the child-molester, opened the proceedings with a brisk knee-up to mangle the testicles, threatening to cut the appendage off so he wouldn't use it again, went. He went burbling protest; but he went. Charlie looked as though his knee still had quick-rising elasticity.

When they were in the car, as Charlie eased it along the narrow lane and on to the road leading to town, he said: 'Didn't think you'd want to drink in your own local.' Truth was, he didn't want to make himself conspicuous in company with a gardener so close to the big house. People in country pubs remember. 'It's real nice to see you again. Does your old guv'nor know you was in the nick?'

'He—he—I—' said Ollie; and stopped. Again, Charlie's sharpness gave him the answer. Ollie's stammering merely confirmed what he had believed: that no rich old man having a house filled with valuable merchandise is likely to subscribe rosily to the Prisoners' After-care Society. The man's being here had to be bent in itself, if only to the extent of forged references, or something of the like. Another possibility—this, too, Charlie had considered—was that he had been planted. By somebody else with all that loot in mind, as man on the inside.

He asked: 'How long you been working there?'

'T—two years.'

'Uh-huh.' Satisfactory answer. He was here long before the hijack attempt, and had he been involved he'd have been done with the rest, or he'd have scarpered. And no organization keeps a man planted for two whole years. That's too long. So it was forged references or whatever; and he must have come here soon after his release. It all meant that he was extremely vulnerable. 'Come here straight from Strangeways, did you? You'd have come out about that time, wouldn't you?'

'I wasn't in—I never been to Strangeways—'

'Oh, come on, Ollie. You don't have to be like that with me. I was there with you, remember? I was in your cell. Shocking, the overcrowding inside these days, ain't it? I blame the telly, it's all these bloody amateurs, bop an old lady over the nut and in they go. Relax, cock, you're among friends. I may even have a proposition for you. Business proposition, could do you a bit of good. Put a bit of poppy in your sky, to buy sweeties for little girls.' The car turned into the main road, running sweetly down into town.

CHAPTER 7

At five-thirty (approx) Detective-Inspector Rosher said to Freddie Lugge, sat with aching hams still upon the hard little chair: 'Do you know what, Freddie? You're being a very silly feller. You're wasting a lot of our time and making it hard for yourself. *We* know you done her—*you* know you done her. We're going to knock off now, give you time to think. You'll be down in our little underground dungeon, when you realize what's good for you just rattle the bars. And if you think today's been hard, just think what tomorrow can bring. All right, Sergeant, see our little friend down the stairs, will you? I'll be up in the Chief's office.'

So Detective-Sergeant Boggis took Freddie away, down to cold and echoing under-regions; while the inspector mounted the stairs and tapped upon the Chief Constable's door. 'Enter,' came an encouraging cry. Rosher entered.

'Ah, Mr Rosher,' said the Chief. 'And how does it go?'

'I'm knocking off for now, sir. He's dug his heels in. We'll give him time to think.'

'Good. Good.' The Chief had called into the interview room during Freddie's interrogation. Spent a little time there, leaning against the wall and listening. Left very quietly, not wishing to interrupt. When he was gone Rosher turned again to tearing up the rule-book, suspended while he was present. 'Should we—er—have allowed him a solicitor, do you think?'

'He can have one tomorrow, sir, if he decides to cooperate. I think it would hamper us right now.' Stiffly spoken. Leave the bugger swinging, no lifeline to grab at. Show him the power of the police, who can deny a suspect almost anything, so long as it can be presented that granting it would hamper them in their enquiries.

'Mm. Hmm. Whatever you think best.' Freddie had asked for his solicitor very early on, and again, because he knew the man leaning on the wall would be top brass, while the Chief was there. Rosher vetoed it; more gently the second time than the first, when he had the interviewee entirely to himself. The Chief would have granted the request; but a good leader, having appointed a man to a position of authority, does not undermine that man by reversing his decisions. Reasonable, the grounds for refusal, it's often done. 'Per—er—Mr Fillimore 'phoned. His back hasn't improved much, apparently. He's resting at home, rather keen to hear how things are going. If you'd like to give him a tinkle you can use my phone.'

Rosher had no desire whatever to give Percy a tinkle; but however he phrases it, when the top man makes speech like that it comes close as dammit to being an order. 'Right,' he said, and crossed to the desk to pick up the telephone.

Downstairs, the lady policeman dutying at the switchboard shoved a plug into a little hole. Rosher dialled. Percy's thin voice came, filtered from the phone beside his bed. It had a sterilizing pad fixed to the mouthpiece and another at the other end, to ward off things that creep in through the ear.

Without conjuring even a fringe of his telephone manner, Rosher said: 'Ah. Rosher here. You wanted to know how things are going. We've arrested him.' Without your help, thank you very much.

'So I understand,' said Percy, who had reached for his phone the moment he heard of the arrest, in South Kensington English, from the BBC news-reader.

'You can reckon the case is cleared.'

'Has he confessed?'

'Not yet. But he will. I've just put him to bed for the night.'

Listening, well aware of Rosher's stiffness and, although he could not distinguish the words—was trying not to listen, actually. A gentleman does not hang an ear towards private telephone conversation—the Chief thought: Pity. Complete personality clash. Both good policemen, in their different ways. Should make a fine team, but put them together and they tend to nullify each other. Pity. Perhaps I should revert to the old system, keep them working apart. But it's not always possible.

Percy was saying: 'Personally, I always prefer to press on. Crack them in one session, keep changing the approach.' Different officers, he meant, himself chief among them; bringing unsettling attitudes with them, from overbearing contempt to let's-have-a-cigarette-I-want-to-be-your-friend.

Well, it's a tried and productive technique; but when Rosher had control it wasn't his way, and Percy knew it. Rosher took sole command, browbeating, cajoling, sending the subject below, having him brought suddenly up again. Holding little shocks back so that he could shake a shoulder in the middle of the night and administer them there and then, appearing like Demon King to the opening eyes, bulky by the narrow cell bed. Let it be said that this bogeyman technique is equally productive. Most people judiciously mix the methods.

Now the inspector visibly seethed. He tried, in deference to the Chief, to smooth the bark out of his voice; but it was there when he said: 'That's the difference. I don't.'

A knock on the door. The Chief's invitation. In came Boggis, to stand just inside. Percy was snapping. 'Yes. Well—you have the case, there's nothing I can do about it.'

Abruptly Inspector Rosher put the phone into its cradle. He then drew out his flourishing off-white handkerchief and raised it to his flaring nostrils. The Chief braced. Sergeant Boggis leaned his weight forward slightly, balancing nicely, with legs apart, on the balls of his feet. Came a mighty rending of calico, reverberating through the panelled office among a whirl of dust motes. Even penetrating the walls, so that a passing lady police-man clutched to her leaping serge bosom the report she was carrying and ejaculated: 'Christ!'

The inspector mopped up, replaced his handkerchief; coughed; extended a thick forefinger to scratch the tenpenny-piece spot of durable skull that pinkened his short-back-and-sides haircut at the crown.

Relaxing, the Chief said: 'What are your plans for the night, Mr Rosher?'

'Sleep here, sir. He'll probably crack before long.' Around three o'clock in the morning, probably, when morale sags to its lowest ebb. Common time for confessions. No point in going home to the lonely and increasingly squalid house on the hill, getting up to dress and hurry back at the strident bidding of the phone.

'Splendid.' The Chief knew enough about Rosher's domestic situation to understand that even when no call of duty demanded it, he would sooner be here than there. Here was the canteen, easy eating on call and often— now, certainly—a legitimate item on the expense sheet, with the washing-up done by somebody paid for it. Here was the true centre of his manhood. And the truckle-bed, though narrow, was very clean-sheeted. CID men draw no double-time and they work erratic hours; but it was not dedication entirely that kept the inspector here very often, long after he was free to depart.

Sergeant Boggis was differently fixed, he had a house with a smallish garden and a buxom wife within. So the Chief added: 'Not necessary for you to stay, though, Sergeant, I think? A few hours off—decent bath and so on—all work and no play, eh? Fix it between yourselves, turn and turn about. All right, gentlemen—thank you. Jolly good day's work.' He smiled and nodded his encouraging nod, to signify that the session was over. Rosher could do as he wished; but that should ensure that young Boggis had a little taste of home cooking.

The two burly men tramped down the stairs. They really were very alike, from behind. There was even the merest hint of thinning on the crown of the sergeant's similar haircut, where a similar tonsure would gleam, given time.

The inspector said: 'You first, then. Don't have to come back if you don't want to, I can ring if I need you.'

'Right,' said Boggis; who would come back, because when a confession is made the names of the officers present are entered on the official report, and he did not intend to be crowded out at the death. It looks bad, to be allocated and closely involved, and then to be missing at the moment of clearing. Rosher, he knew, was fully capable of calling in any old copper as witness if the subject confessed, letting the phone call ride while he, Boggis, slept his way into dubious conduct. The Old Man said time off, turn and turn about. Yes—he'd be back.

Now, though, he turned aside at the first landing to enter the big and by no means unpleasant canteen. I will have, he thought, a couple of quick light ales before I go; because the truth is, he was not quite so joyfully married as people believed, and so in no pressing hurry to be home.

Seven years he'd been married, and the itch was

rearing; but in his wife, rather than in himself. Many a CID man's wife finds herself itching, long before the acceptable seven years is up, to throw rocks at his head, or to smash up all the furniture, or to open up to any bloody man who comes this way, provided he's not a policeman. It's his erratic working time that does it, plus the fact that a man of brawn and muscle absorbed willy-nilly in his job is rarely a good lover. Then there is the social isolation meted out to the wife of any copper. And disillusion, when having married in the belief that he will share with her the high drama and glamour of being a detective and the social respect going with it, she finds him too often withdrawn and preoccupied in a world far from glamour, and eyed rather suspiciously by the neighbours, all of whom have a guilty conscience about something or other. It puts her out on the limb beside him, and it's a rare woman who enjoys it.

So he drank two light ales, which occupied him until about five minutes to six; when he trod away to his car, parked on the station forecourt, and set off for home. As he reached the corner of the street he looked right; looked left; and waited, because a car was coming along having right of way. In it, as it approached, he found somebody he knew from his big city days. Charlie Palkin, driving along with a bearded character beside him.

Hallo, hallo, hallo, he thought: what's that little bugger doing here? Passing through, or stopping? If stopping—up to a caper? With the geezer under the whiskers?

So who's the geezer with the whiskers? Local boy? Or come in with Charlie from out of town? Called upon for a job?

Well—she doesn't know I'm coming home, so she's not going to kick. Might as well follow 'em a little way, see if there's anything to sniff at. The little sod didn't spot me. And he turned his car, to follow the other at a discreet distance; which is the right thing to do, really. No copper, of course, can follow every crook he sees whenever he goes out; but a new face on a manor is always worth inspection.

They drove a very little way, not more than three or four hundred yards, before the Palkin car turned in to the car park of the Black Bull. Two vehicles behind—never tread on the heel of the man being tailed—Sergeant Boggis arrived; in time to see, very definitely, that here was Charlie Palkin, walking into the plusher of the bars with his hand behind the elbow of a bearded man who seemed not over-anxious to go.

There was no radio in Boggis's car, and his walkie was back at the station; but a phone booth stood on the kerb across the road from the Black Bull. He entered and sported a fivepenny piece to tell the duty lady, in case he was needed in a hurry, where he was breaking his journey. Call him here, the number was in the book. And tell the landlord to be discreet, passing the message on. Then he followed his subjects into the pub, making a mental note that five pence was to go on his expenses. Things like that get forgotten, and they add up.

It's a fine inn, the Black Bull, very old and tipsy, wearing its red-tiled roof a trifle awry, as if centuries of rising fume from rollicking Saturday nights has gone to its happy head. A little bit tarted, of course, being right in the town centre facing the wide-open, cobbled market square, but not intolerably so. Hunting prints on the walls and a few old photographs showing local events happening long ago, outside. A painting or two of the magpie façade, done by travelling artists of varying talent. No juke-box, no television, no tinging and pinging ball machines. It's a pub, the real-ale-crusty landlord says to whoever is fool enough to ask if, tucked away somewhere, there is not a little bar possessing these common delights. It's a pub, he says, not a whorehouse.

If you want a whorehouse, there's one in Charlton Street. There is, too.

There are two bars only: a large one serving those whose main interest is in real ale and a dartboard; and a smaller one, called The Snug, for people who pay a couple of pennies per pint more for the pleasures of utter decorum and privacy. Into the larger went Boggis, finding two darts devotees and a serious ale-man there; but not Charlie Palkin and the man with the beard. No disappointment in this—he had seen the beard escorted into the Snug and had deliberately chosen the main bar, knowing that so early in the evening the smaller would have few if any other patrons in it. He knew Charlie, Charlie knew him. It would never do, lurching conspicuously in to stand breathing all over the man.

Up came the landlord, ale-nourished nose and all. One wall eye, the other like a pickled fried egg. He said: 'Evening, Mr Boggis. Drop of the Home Brew?'

Boggis put an unobtrusive finger to his lips. From where he sat at the bar he could see in an angled mirror, and not by accident, right through the service hatch into the Snug, where Charlie and the bearded man sat in the fireside alcove. Charlie was smiling, an ingratiating smile; and talking. The bearded man sat stiffly, radiating no happiness. 'Keep it down, Ted,' the sergeant murmured. 'Who's the bloke with the whiskers?'

'What bloke?' the landlord said in a lowered voice. The darts devotees played on, engrossed. The ale-man nursed his pint by the diamond-paned window, savouring deeply after the barren hours between lunch-time closing and evening opening.

'In the Snug.'

'Don't know. Never seen him before. Bent, is he?'

'That remains to be seen. Yes—give us a pint. Home Brew.' Another item for the expense sheet.

The landlord drew white-collared perfection and went

away, his pickled-egg eye inclining now to stray Snugward. Boggis took an appreciative swig and kept his casual eyes on the mirror, a rim of pure white suds around his mouth. His own reflection did not appear in it, and wouldn't to viewers in the little bar. Cunningly angled, that mirror, by a publican who likes to know what is happening in both rooms without seeming to pry. I wish I could hear what the little bastard's saying, Boggis thought.

Charlie, in fact, had covered fair ground during the journey down. He beat about few bushes, because to capitalize shock it is best to hammer on; especially when you know you hold a very pliable whip. As Charlie did. He was using it now.

'Wouldn't be difficult, Ollie, old mate, would it? We can soon hire a couple of little girls who'd swear your life away. Your record, fake references and all, who's going to believe you didn't get up to the old how's-yer-farver in your little cottage? Don't think we couldn't do it, send 'em down here on the bus for a day trip. Have 'em come screaming out of your cottage with their knickers round their knees. Not very nice inside, is it, getting belted all the time because you're a dirty little pervert? Well, then—you ain't going to tell anybody what I'm going to tell you, are you? We're giving you the choice, see? You can go back inside, and we've got very rough friends in there, too. Or you go free as a bird, poppy in your sky to spend on sweeties.'

A long silence, during which Charlie leaned back, supping at his pint, and Boggis watched. Also supping, because Home Brew is so good a beer that the glass rises to the lips unbidden, until the drinker finds with surprise that it is empty. The bearded man spoke. Very briefly. Boggis knew he spoke by the upcoming of his head, the small wag of his bushy beard. What he said brought satisfaction to Charlie. So it seemed, by the reburgeoning of his smile. Actually, the brief speech told Charlie he was in.

Ollie said: 'How much poppy?'

'Well, now—that depends on how much you do for us. I'd say you can count on five hundred nicker.' Make it a tempting figure. It might never be paid. On the other hand: if the geezer was *really* useful, five hundred was peanuts. He wasn't going to be hard to handle—he was shit-scared they'd shop him.

Yes, Ollie was scared; but on a much deeper level than Charlie knew. He hadn't meant to kill her—God knows, he didn't mean to—

'Think of it, Ollie boy. Think what you can do, with five hundred smackers.'

Ollie was thinking of it. The only reason he was still in the town was, quite simply, that he had so little money. Rent-free accommodation sounds very fine, but it means, when a parsimonious employer can get away with it, a pittance wage; and Ollie, after a demoralizing spell of unemployment following his release from Strangeways, presenting false references supplied by a man recommended by a man inside, was in no condition to argue terms. What he needed at that moment was not union wages but a job; and with this one went a Godsent cottage to live in, away from people. He feared people with a fear that mounted to phobia under the brutal experience of arrest, and trial, and Strangeways.

This fear, of men and particularly—at least until he went to prison and came up against that traditional code of violence towards child molesters—of women, all spreading from guilt at his own sexuality, is the common fruit of upbringing in a house devoted to one of the more virulently thunderous religious sects. His parents were strict and implacable worshippers of a vengeful, sexually bent and venomous God. Solitary, terrified masturbation with an eye on the bedroom door or locked away in the lavatory does not make for easy relations with the opposite sex.

He had never known a woman; and nature, when a man is shut away from love by fear, will increase desire in an effort to drive him into decreed consummation. This collision between fear and desire made of Ollie, when he got a job as school caretaker, sitting duck for naughty little girls; of whom there are many. A man frightened by women often feels less terrified with children. Psychologists' truism.

And now he was a killer, his one desire to get away before the rough, contemptuous police who put him away last time found out that the man they arrested yesterday (he heard it on the wireless) was not the one who did it, and arrived to tap him on the shoulder; as he'd thought this man had, being one of them. All his instincts said: Flee; but the core of his thinking brain said: How far will you get, without money? They'll know it was you, as soon as they know you've gone; which Mrs Rummidge will tell them. Of course she will, if you're missing.

Now here was this man, this terrible, violent man reinforcing his need to flee; threatening him with return to where brutal men would terrorize him again, screws not present or looking the other way; and offering money. Money enough. 'What would I—have to do?' he muttered.

Sergeant Boggis, feeling by now the press upon his bladder, saw Charlie's smile positively radiate. Sod it, he thought—if I could only hear what's going on. Bloody frustrating. Can't even lip-read, the bastard's using the old lag delivery, out of the side of the mouth.

Charlie was saying: 'Now you're being sensible. It's dead easy—no problem at all. All we want from you is a bit of cooperation. Have you got a key?'

'Key?'

'To the house. The big house.'

'Oh. No.'

Sod it. Too much to expect, but it would have made the job so very simple. Charlie was a wizard on alarm systems; but locks he didn't like. Too often, without a special key they go off in clamour or buzz the local police station before you can get inside to do something about it.

'Ah. Well—you have to go into the house?'

'I take vegetables in every morning. And I have a cup of coffee at eleven. With Mrs Rummidge. In the kitchen.'

'Rummidge?'

'The housekeeper.'

'Ah. So how do you get in?'

'You're going to burgle it.'

'Oh, for Christ's sake! What did you think we was going to do, repaper the fucking walls? What do you think we're going to pay you all that money for?'

'I can't—burgle—'

'You silly bugger, you don't have to. You don't even have to be *near* the place. All we need is information. Like layout of the rooms. Where the cellar door is. And I want to be let in. That's all. We'll do the rest.'

In the bigger bar, Sergeant Boggis was thinking: I'll have to have a piss. Very soon.

They were silent now in the little bar. Thinking, by the look of it, was being done. The beard waggled again. I'm a silly bugger, the sergeant thought—I shouldn't have had this pint on top of those light ales, when it works through I'll be desperate. But a man can't sit at a bar and not have a drink handy. Not if he wants to be inconspicuous. And it's a helluva good beer.

'You can get in. It's burglar alarms, isn't it? You're bothered about 'em going off.'

'Clever,' said Charlie. 'No mug, our Ollie. Get me in, I can fix 'em. But it's tricky, from the outside.'

'You can get in. Mrs Rummidge has 'em turned off all day.'

'What?'

'She turns them off when she gets up. Puts 'em back on when she goes to bed.'

Easy enough, most systems work from a master switch. But—bloody hell. All that loot, all day long, and no alarm cover? 'You sure?' said Charlie.

'Yes, she told me. I play Monopoly with her sometimes, in the evenings. Can't fiddle about all the time, she says, so they don't go off every time she opens a door or window. So she switches them off. She reckons there's nothing there now that anybody'd want to steal.'

Ah—but she doesn't know what we know. 'What about old Sir Roland? Does he let her do it?'

'He doesn't know. She reckons he's barmy, anyway. Nothing to pinch and he wants it all locked in. He never comes out of his room.'

'Stone me,' said Charlie. A piece of cake. A plate of veritable clam chowder. 'So—how do you get me in?'

'I—I—I can't—'

'D'you remember Spider Biltmore? Big feller—you ought to, he smashed you in the mouth. He's in again. Wonder if you'll come across him?'

'I've got a key to the conservatory.'

'Where's that?'

'At the back of the house. But there's an inside door before you get into the house.'

'You're a good boy. You just get me into the conservatory.' Given private time, no particular need to fear locks. It's getting through them in a hurry makes the real danger, when you must do it in the open. In the country particularly. You're noticeable by day, and a torch shines at night like a beacon. 'What's it like, this door?'

I'll have to have one, Boggis was thinking, if I'm to stick with these two. What happens if they take off and I have to follow? I piss myself, that's what; or stop and lose 'em.

'Just a door.'

'Not steel, anything like that?'

'No. Just wood. I go in that way.'

Slip out now, thought Sergeant Boggis. He left the bar counter, bound for a door marked Gents let into the wall to his right.

'Ollie, boy,' said Charlie, 'you've just come into five hundred green 'uns. That's my way in.'

'Ah. When are you—?'

'What's wrong with now?' Sooner the better. Get in quick, before somebody else did. If it wasn't as simple as it sounded—and could it be? Was it possible?—one could always draw back. Gambler's instinct, in which Charlie trusted, as do most of the bent, said grab it while it's here. 'Drink up, it's your lucky day.'

When the sergeant returned he looked at once into the mirror. Nobody now in the small snug, just two empty glasses standing on the table. Into his mind leaped language the public believes policemen never use; except on television, where they rush about indulging in behaviour which would see your actual copper out, slithering along on his bum.

The landlord approached, mumbling low. Landlords like to stand well with the police. 'They just left, Mr Boggis. I saw 'em through the window—down towards Bondgate.' Even the wall-eye looked furtive. But eager.

'Ta.' Boggis moved rapidly out from the pub, thinking: That helps. Because Bondgate lies on the opposite side of the market square from the Black Bull, and you can turn either way along it. Whichever you choose, right or left, there are forks of equal stature leading out of town, and side streets galore.

He drove to Bondgate; but Charlie's car was gone. So he went home; had a wash and a smidgeon of supper; kissed his wife, who was comely but growing more and more petulant, and returned to the station; where,

having nothing to do anyway, he looked through the
Rogues' Gallery, seeking likeness of the bearded man.
Well before he closed the last bulky file, of course,
Charlie was inside the inadequately guarded home of that
tightwad old reprobate Sir Roland Goyt. Knighted,
would you believe it, for services to the nation. Invented
and supplied, at a huge profit, a new and improved
flame-thrower to fry people with.

When they were retiring for the night, Rosher and
Boggis, in the little room at the station equipped with two
camp beds kept ready for just such occasions—and duty
makes strange bedfellows—the sergeant said: 'Do you
have a client with a bushy beard? Dark hair, looks like a
manual worker, around five foot eight. Nervous look
about him.'

'Not much of a description,' Rosher grunted. 'Why?'

'Saw one of my old clients, name of Charlie Palkin.
From the city. He was with this geezer with the beard. I
was wondering if they're up to something.'

Rosher grunted again. 'They're all up to something.
Let's get the bloody light out.' And I wouldn't mind
betting, he was thinking, you snore like a pig all night.

Pity. Two little light ales. If Boggis had eschewed them
he might well have tagged the bearded man and killed
two birds there and then, in a blaze of glory. A little
circumspect creeping and he could have returned to the
station with Charlie and Ollie both in tow. It would have
saved so much trouble.

But then, he had no idea what Ollie had done, who he
was and where he came from. And Rosher had glimpsed
him only once, rear view as he mowed the lawn. Backlit at
that, in the piebald sunshine. Pity.

CHAPTER 8

Charlie got into the house so easily that to the adrenal in-race of his blood was added bubbles of excited laughter that threatened to jump out through his nostrils in little explosive snorts. The keyed-up mind tends to react immoderately, and however experienced a man, at the moment of action he finds himself and all his senses supercharged with that kick of adrenalin.

This fine transcending of mundane matter can hook a man as surely, and disastrously, as any other drug. Actors starve to get it, and commit suicide, directly or by bottle, when it eludes them. Soldiers who have known it, dying from the boredom of peace, pray for war again. The villain who retires, or tries to go straight, is called back often by the need for it, rather than for loot. Many are the impecunious bent who wabble from porridge to National Assistance and back to porridge, leaving women and children to shift as best they may, because they can't give it up.

Charlie loved it. It hooked him as a child, stuffing goodies up his jumper in shops. He was hooked still, and forever, feeling fully alive only when cloaked in silent, throbbing darkness; all the world around sleeping except for his co-workers, while he fixed a system and turned to help with the gathering-in. Now he stood alert and utterly fulfilled, forcing back these little snorts of astonished hilarity.

All the gear Ernie Parvis reckoned was stowed away here, and you could get in from the conservatory with a bent pin. Ollie Hardcastle, cowering now in his cottage, had been right: the door from the conservatory into the house was of wood, with a simple mortice lock, reinforced by a Yale set further up. Not even bolted, no chains; and when he tested the alarm system before opening it was dead. The old girl, it seemed, really did turn it all off.

What a turn-up for the book! If he'd known about it he needn't have touched Ollie at all. Better if he hadn't, really. Keep it all tight. But who'd have expected it, even though Ernie said the old bastard's so mean he won't even trim his fingernails in case he loses the clippings. You'd think he'd spend a bob or two on a guard or two, wouldn't you, even if they doubled as butlers? And something better than a two-wire system that a silly old bint turned off all day? Well—praise God from whom all blessings flow.

He picked up his small case, which held many interesting little articles apart from what was left of the sandwiches and coffee, and refastened the ineffectual locks. Then he tiptoed away, passing the kitchen with the light showing under the door and on across the hall; to that broom closet into which Rosher walked during his visit here.

Plenty of space inside, he'd had bedrooms smaller. He settled down to wait quite happily. About eleven, Ollie said, the housekeeper went up. Half an evening away; but as well be here early as passing time in pubs. Never drink before work; and if you are in unknown territory, keep under cover if you can. He might have gone back to his hotel room; but night porters notice, if you leave again late and don't return until much later. He was all right here, with his sandwiches and a little fruit.

Ollie was right again. At ten o'clock precisely he heard the kitchen door open quiet, this house, as a deaf-mutes' singsong—and a mutter pass up the stairs. Alone, Mrs Rummidge tended to mutter, so that in spite of the muffling of her slipper-scuff by carpet, Charlie could tell roughly where she was. Bang on time—according to Ollie, at ten she took Sir Roland's supper up. Thin toast

and something hot in a mug, called Beefox and said to be
stuffed with vitamins, minerals and other carefully
balanced nutrients intended to bring the old and infirm
to a rickety gallop. At five past the hour she came down,
still muttering, and shut herself back in the kitchen, there
to consume cocoa and a little of what she fancied. Charlie
ate a banana.

At eleven she came again, going this time to the front
door (he watched her here through the keyhole) to lock it,
bolt it and hang it with a chain; to the back door; to the
smaller back door, the one connecting the house with the
conservatory. All bolts shot, all locks fast and chains *in
situ*, she shuttered the windows; and again he could
watch while she dealt with the stained-glass leaded lights
in the hall, one on each side of the great door. He
strained an ear at the keyhole to hear what she was
muttering; but all it gathered was rhubarb, rhubarb,
rhubarb.

Now she went again towards the back of the house—to
the head of the cellar steps, he knew, where the main
electric switches were. Ollie had been there twice, to
change a fuse for her when her electric iron went spttz.
And now she muttered herself away up the stairs again.
This time, she stayed there.

Charlie gave it half an hour. Then he came out, and
for some while, working by well-shielded torchlight, he
did things that had better be left as a trade secret. We
don't want everybody at it.

The old man had splurged more on defence for the
main front and back entrances. He had electric eyes
dotted about, and a few other gadgets as well as the wired
system; but purely child's stuff. And so easily disarmed.
As soon as Charlie had located them all he simply moved
to the cellarhead and turned the lot off. Thus, he could
screw away here, shove a little bit of plastic there, cut
through this and reconnect to that without the slightest

chance of their going uproarious. Then he turned the main switch on again. Simple as that.

When he had done these things he went down into the cellar. Not to tamper with anything, but because while he was here he might as well have a glinny at it, so that he could tell Leonard how it looked. It would be expected of him.

The stone slab flooring fitted together perfectly, you would have sworn it had remained undisturbed since the house was built. But Ernie had marked which of these slabs was hinged, with the goodies beneath, and behind which of the wall blocks the triggering mechanism lurked. No problem. Charlie turned and moved wraithlike back up the stairs; coming face to face with Sir Roland as he turned the corner into the passage. He switched his torch on; and out of the air came a Jacob Marley face, goggling like a nutcracker and gasping—well, so was Charlie— from the shock. No more than four yards away.

Nobody had told Charlie—nobody knew, except possibly Mrs Rummidge—that the old buzzard, tormented by the terror normal among nutcracker-jawed and senile multi-millionaires, spent his nights with eyes wide open like those of a decrepit lizard, listening for the noises in the night that would mean thieves broken in, or police, or Customs men; or all at once; to cart away his treasure. Often he got up in the dark. Left his room, crept down the stairs to check that all was well.

This is what he'd done now. Shuffled in his dressing-gown—quietly, quietly; he didn't want Mrs Rummidge to suspect that anything special lay in the cellar, she was no more to be trusted than anybody else in the whole wide world, into the crust of which his products had put so many dents—down the stairs; and zoop! As he turned the corner a torch-beam hit him right in the eyes. Dimly he could see a face behind it; and seeing it, forthwith he shuffled the other foot into the grave and fell down dead.

Now Charlie was a long-service pro, by no means given to panic. It leaped up in him when the ghastly, ghostly face hung there suddenly, glimmering like a starveling, pop-eyed doorknocker; but when the terrible thing dropped, quite suddenly with a soft thud, he bit down on the urge to fly and disciplined his quivering limbs to advance; until he stood close to the huddled little shrunken body and said in a whisper:

'You all right?'

Not a clever speech. An old man does not go down plop in his nightshirt if he is all right; but Charlie was not seeking applause. He was very badly shaken, instinct still battling for its running rights, professionalism denying them. He bent, to feel for a pulse; and what he said now was:

'Christ Almighty—he's dead.'

He knew, although they had never met, that this had to be Sir Roland. The late Sir Roland, on his way suddenly to God to explain about that flame-thrower and sundry other gadgetry. Fixed with adrenalin, the mind works with supra-normal clarity and speed. Almost as it impinged upon him that the old man was dead he knew what he must do.

He bent; lifted the carcase, which wasn't difficult; a diet of prunes, thin toast and Beefox will reduce much more solid bodies swiftly to skin and bone; and carried it up the stairs, praying that Mrs Rummidge—who slept on the floor above, Ollie said—would not feel the need to come down, to make water or cut herself a slice of fruitcake, final snack before sleep.

Nothing stirred. A door stood open. Big bedroom. Big bed, crumpled. This had to be it. Charlie carried his burden through—strange how a body flops. It seems, suddenly, all lolling head, and arms, and legs. You no sooner get one limb gathered as it tries to flop away than another starts sliding—and insinuated the late Sir Roland back into his bed and left him there, lying prone with the bedclothes up to his chin, his ancient-tortoise, gum-naked mouth open, his reptile eyes glaring up at the ceiling until Charlie, feeling it would look better, closed the lids with his thumbs before he tiptoed away; down the stairs, along that passage to the back door; and out to fresh air, via the conservatory.

He did not call in to the cottage, where Ollie cowered. He walked, and quite a long way—silly to park too close—to his car, left at the top of the long hill that leads away from town and goes to the big city. He got in and freewheeled down for nearly a mile before he let the clutch out to make the engine catch without the attention-inviting whirr of the starter motor. And he drove straight home.

Didn't even ring Leonard. That could wait until morning. Operators at night are often bored and listening in. The small hours had arrived by now, and he found his clothes wringing with sweat. So he showered, and went to bed.

Another day came, bright and beautiful and pacing itself nicely. Morning lambs leaped high in the air and came down in daisies. All the flowers in meadow and garden smiled through dew and nodded at the breeze. Trees pushed on with leaf-making and sap-rising, in the usual last-minute panic in case they'd left it too late. Squirrels woke up and wondered where in heck they left the nuts. Cows twitched tails provocatively like fan-dancers' tassels, and watching bulls made snorting-randy began to paw the ground, impatient to begin the day's work. Even Sergeant Boggis awoke in his camp bed with an erection; which he hid from Inspector Rosher, who was rarely so decked these days.

No call had come bidding them attend upon confessing Freddie; who had spent a terrible night of fret and worry,

lying on the lumpy bunk in a stuffily chill cell, which
opened twice around midnight to permit the pouring in
of two rumbustious drunks. That is how crowded conditions are nowadays: even a man in Freddie's position
cannot look forward to privacy.

By the time the key of the early-duty policeman grated
in the lock he had decided to make a clean breast of
everything: his pressing of the key-imprint (he should
have kept it, he shouldn't have flushed it away) designed
to facilitate entry into the house—everything. If they
believed him—and why would he murder the girl, having
got what he wanted?—perhaps he could turn Queen's
Evidence. Vanish afterwards, before Leonard could
arrange to have him chivvied, or altered with acid; or
even—oh, he should never have become embroiled—
cemented and dropped into deep water somewhere.
Yes—yes—he'd bare his entire breast. But in the presence
of his solicitor.

The warder-policeman came in, ignoring the two
drunks still lying like the snoring dead. He said: 'You can
have an egg on us, son, or we'll send out to a caff if you
want kippers and caviare. Beautiful morning out there,
you'd be surprised.'

Freddie, who felt no yearning for breakfast, said: 'I
want my solicitor.'

'Now that,' said the copper, 'is beyond my jurisdiction.
Unless you'd like him fried. Our Mr Rosher will be down
soon, no doubt. Take it up with him. I'll bring you an
egg, we can always return it to stock if you don't eat it.'

He brought an egg, with bread and butter and a large
tin mug brimming over with tea so weak it is wonderful
that it had strength enough to slop into the tray. 'Lovely,
ain't it?' he said. 'There's many in the Third World would
think it must be Christmas.'

The meal stood untouched, and one of the drunks lay
groaning and holding his head when the copper came in

again, saying jovially: 'On your feet, my son. Inspector Rosher will see you now. Upstairs.'

Freddie was ushered along the bare stone subterranean passage to the foot of the stone stairs down which his shoes clacked yesterday, and here the policeman handed him over to another, almost identical. This one took him upward, to that beady little interview room; where Detective-Inspector Rosher and Detective-Sergeant Boggis were already arrived, shaved and with their teeth cleaned, furnished inside with eggs and bacon, toast, marmalade and teak tea consumed in the canteen.

'Morning, Alistair,' the inspector said. He was seated at the desk. 'Or are we someone else this morning? Sit down, we're about to embark on the first of many little chats.'

'I want my solicitor.'

There is a sameness of style in the way most policemen address most suspects. A kind of avuncular joviality. The mailed fist shows in the eyes, the velvet glove never quite fits. Now he said: 'All right, son. That's your right. You'll be up before the beak this morning anyway, and you'll have to have him there. Give us his name, we'll lug him out of bed.'

So before Freddie was driven to the magistrates' court—you can walk it in five minutes, but it's embarrassing in handcuffs, with pressmen scudding about—he spent a little time privately with his solicitor. Mr Marks of Marks, Marks, Marks and (truly; it's a common name) Spencer. Bent, if only to the extent that he had acted on Freddie's behalf before, knowing him guilty. And now he gave bad advice.

He said: 'If I were you I should say nothing. At this stage. See what sort of case they're presenting against you.'

CHAPTER 9

When Mrs Rummidge got up, not too early, she did as always. Put in her teeth, put on her robe (quilted; bought at the Thursday Market, and very good value), and slippered along to her lavatory, en suite. After which she padded downstairs, switched off the alarm system, opened the shutters in the kitchen and put the kettle on, attending to the other windows while she waited for it to boil.

She liked this time of day, this rising later than she'd been able to in any previous job; this sitting in a kitchen to all intent and purpose her own, this sipping of the first cup of tea, this dunking of biscuits with the lemon-fresh sun beaming in.

Out there in the springing garden work was afoot already: Ollie Hardcastle, bending to finish the job left yesterday, planting things out for the summer. Half would rot or come puky from sun-starvation, or blow to bits as they did in July last year; but never say die. When the sun shines, get 'em in.

Her cup of tea finished, Mrs Rummidge arose and went back up the stairs to her own private bathroom, replete with oils and deodorant unguents, bath salts and Steradent, where she put off her quilted robe and stood in her pink nightgown to give herself and her teeth a good wash. And then, dressed, back to the kitchen and a solid breakfast. What boots it to be in charge of victualling, if your own breakfast be not solid?

Now came 9.45. The stewed prunes were on the tray, a slice of thin dry toast beside the spoon and little bowl. Pausing only to remove iron clamps from her hair—since Evie went she had to do maid's work as well, and it didn't look as if the stingy old bugger was going to get another—she picked up the tray and carried it upstairs.

Overstatement, to say that she was shocked at finding Sir Roland dead, or even surprised; after all, he'd been tottering on the brink long enough. But she was put out. As who would not be, come so suddenly, on such a lovely morning, face to face with the folding of a very soft number? Bugger it, she thought. Now I'll have to get another job.

She went down the stairs again. Threw prunes and toast and all into the waste disposal unit and set it chomping. Small nourishment it would get from that. Then she went into the hall, to telephone the doctor. And after that, the front door being nigh, she opened it and cried through the bird-whistling air:

'Mr Hardcastle—can you spare a moment?'

Ollie, like Freddie, had spent a dreadful night. The worst in a series stretching back to last Saturday. Freddie did at least toss and turn in some sort of bed. Ollie remained clad, crouched all night in the wooden-armed rocking-chair, property of the estate, who stood it by the gas-fire in his cottage. Once there was a lovely old fireplace there, but progress blocked it in.

He sat in the dark, believing rightly that an isolated cottage lit all night is itemized for chit-chat among poachers and early milkers and any other country person who happens to pass, starved of matter for gossip. From when he showed Charlie the way in to the house, all through the hours up to and beyond the lovely dawn, he sat waiting for the man to return; not seeing that beautiful sunrise, not seeing anything beyond what went on in his head.

And what went on in there was a chaos of new shock added to fear already churning. How did the man know he was here? Had he been tabbed, ever since he left

Strangeways? He wasn't a seasoned criminal, he didn't know how they worked. He didn't know anything. Had they been watching—on Saturday—when he—killed her? And who were *they*?

He'd panicked when the man arrived so shockingly. It was all confusion. Even if they didn't know—if they only knew he was here under false pretences—if they told the police that much—or even Sir Roland—the police would come . . . And he dreaded the police.

Oh, it was all confusion. He'd let the man in—in his fear. The man said they'd fix him—little girls—return him to the hell of violent men, whispering from the side of the mouth what they'd do to him. Doing it, when opportunity offered. Locked in every night, three or four to a cell. Or alone, segregated for his own safety. A narrow bunk, a washbasin, a pisspot and utter silence. And a Bible, thundering his damnation.

He shouldn't have let him in. But—how could he resist this terrible man who had crippled him once with a knee to the groin? And the man offered money. With money, he could get away. Before the police came. They'd find out, they'd know this arrested fellow didn't do it. They were clever, they'd arrive. Suddenly. As the man arrived; panicking his mind into rigid terror, because he'd thought it was them. And he offered money. With five hundred pounds he could get away.

Where was the man? Why didn't he come back?

He didn't mean to kill her. He just—wanted—what the other fellow had.

Ever since she arrived he had thought that perhaps she—Because she wasn't pretty, it was the pretty ones who giggled and challenged and—flaunted. Tormenting. Cruel. Devil-creatures, made in lust to torture men with lust. Even little girls. He'd thought little girls were—different. But they flaunted, too, and giggled when he—did what he did to them. And they kept coming giggling back, to tempt him again. More of them, they brought their friends. Until the police came.

He hadn't done it since. When she arrived he thought perhaps—because she was quiet and—shy. He thought he might—even—one day—even marry. Her.

But he could not properly speak to her. In the night, often and often, he talked to her, caressed her, held her naked and soft and warm in his arms until masturbation brought some kind of ease; but if he met her, in the house when he went to do an odd job or in the garden when she came out, working or on her way to and from the town in her time off, his face refused to smile and his throat closed drily. He would mumble a gruff greeting, feeling his eyes glower to shield himself against her femaleness, feeling his face stiffen under the beard he grew to hide behind when he left prison.

It was purely chance that had taken him to the town on Saturday. He went in very rarely, crowds were not for him. But he needed new cotter pins for his bicycle—he had no car, couldn't drive one; but he cycled, all by himself around and about—on Saturday, so he went to Dawling's, the one shop in town that sells such things.

There is one cinema in the town, and it was showing a film about a war in space and another featuring a monster that looked, from the stills, as if it rose out of crimson molasses, snarling and draped in seaweed, to terrorize the midget crew of a midget ship by tearing it in half. Why go home? he thought. I can have a pie and peas, and catch the last house.

The monster wasn't so good as it looked on the billboard. When he came out he went for a pint to the Three Feathers almost next door. It stands nearly opposite the Laughing Jackass discotheque, and through the window he saw her coming out of there, escorted by a tall, handsome man who took her arm as if she belonged to him, his smiling down at her almost a caress.

A shock of jealousy flamed up in him, green as that other monster. She was smiling back—walking away, her body leaning against the tall, easy man when he pulled her arm through his, patting her hand; speaking intimately out of his handsome lips. She can't, his mind cried out, in an agony. She can't—she can't—

His pint abandoned, as the landlord called time he left the pub and followed, at a distance, along the street called Coppergate, to the park. Had they looked back they might have seen him there by the light of the moon before he reached the point where the wood known simply as The Wood began, fringing the path with cover. But they did not look back. By now, the man had his arm around her and her head was on his shoulder.

Hidden in a bush, he saw all that happened beside the lake, half sobbing with agony, blasting to rage when the man kissed her; moved a hand to her breast while she responded urgently. Then the man whispered; rose from the seat; took her hand, smiling and murmuring; coaxing; brought her gently to stand before him; took her in his arms and kissed her again, long and lingering, and she pressing her body close while he fondled her breast with one hand, the other moving on her back, moving to her buttocks.

And now the man whispered again; and they were coming this way, his arm around her, his hand cupping her, playing still with her small teat.

Too late now for Ollie to move unobserved, even if he had been disposed to try. His bush was on the lake side of a clearing, one of the fringe that hid it from open view. He saw the man bring her to within a few feet; saw them lie down; saw her slim, white legs unveiled as the moving hand slowly stroked upward, pushing back the yellow frock. Saw him unbutton her so that he could push aside the bra to kiss her nipples; and she gasping, moaning. Saw her move to assist removal of her knickers, and the small dark triangle and white belly; saw her legs part under the stroking and the man move to bring himself between.

Almost, it was the man that Ollie killed—poor Freddie, who would have leaped up and run like the clappers, had he known. Almost, he bounded upon them to destroy; but in the core of his terrible tumult, fascinated voyeurism was holding him now. He had never seen . . . His eyes watched the man fumble; he heard her short, ecstatic-hurt gasp as she was entered; heard her moaning as Freddie's buttocks moved; heard her glad, whimpering cries—she climaxed sooner than Freddie—and the man's grunting, the shortening of his breath before he pumped urgently, and collapsed upon her.

She moved, almost at once; too shaken, too self-embroiled to fall into the good swoon that follows comfortable passion. His erection hard upon him, Ollie saw now her awkward redonning of underwear, her buttoning and the straightening of her hair, the man sitting beside her and brushing fastidiously at his suit with the hands that lately roamed her.

They moved out, when they were up and on their feet, through the gap on the opposite side of the clearing. It brought them on to the dirt track leading one way to the lake, the other through the wood. The man kissed her again; spoke a little; watched as she turned to walk away. She left him abruptly—mark, although Ollie didn't know it, of the confusion in her—taking the longer path. The man watched until she rounded the bend before he turned back the way they came.

Ollie moved now. She was just like all the rest—she was just like all the rest. Deceitful—depraved—doing it under bushes, anywhere—animal—lust. All demure, all primly shy—the whore. Anybody—do it with anybody—anywhere. Lust—lust. She was just like all the rest.

The path winds. It leads to the gates on the opposite

side of the park. Cross a few fields from here and you arrive in the lane that leads to Notley House. Ollie walked it often, but she never did after dark. But then, never before had she missed the last bus.

She came round a bend and found him standing bulky in the path just by the glen where her body was found, and was afraid at once even before she recognized him.

She said: 'What—what—who—?'

'You cow,' he said.

Now she knew him. 'What—what—what do you want?'

He moved forward to grip her arms and she tugged away, two staggering sideway paces that pulled him with her into the glen; crying: 'Go away—go away—I'll tell Mrs Rummidge . . .'

'I want—I want—' he said, unable to frame it. One hand leaped down and up under her skirt. As she jerked her pelvis backward he felt the softness of her pubes under his hand and the nylon give as he lunged the thin pants downward, clumsily because of his fear and his inexperience. She opened her mouth to scream.

'Don't—don't—' he said; and—oh, it was all a nightmare—the next thing he knew clearly was her choking, and her body sagging down; to the grass, when he let her go. And he only meant to stop her screaming.

Crouching, shaking her, he knew that she was dead. He was half way home before he found that he had brought her handbag with him. Did he pick it up? Why would he do that? He didn't know, it was all unreal, a confused nightmare.

Now he looked up from planting out chrysanthemums in a spring-bright bed, heart-leap catching his breath as Mrs Rummidge appeared at the door of the house and cried: 'Mr Hardcastle—can you spare a moment?'

They're here, he thought. It's a trick—they're in there. The police—they've sent her out to entice me in.

But—she was coming out, to stand at the foot of the steps.

He rose from his cramped gardening posture. Moved across the pool-table lawn with the trowel still in his hand.

She said, soberly when he came near enough: 'Mr Hardcastle, I'm afraid I've got bad news for you.'

'Ah,' he said.

She arranged her face into stained-glass-window pietism. 'I'm afraid,' she said, 'Sir Roland has gone beyond.'

CHAPTER 10

At almost the same time when Leonard Figgis, at a hastily convened conference, arrived at his big decision, Detective-Inspector Rosher set out with Sergeant Boggis to stand Frederick Sidney Lugge up before the magistrate.

This did not take long. They drove to the courthouse in an official car, the two policemen in the front with Boggis driving, Freddie handcuffed in the back beside his solicitor; who excused himself to make a phone call while they waited in the bleak reception corridor separate from the one wherein gloomed and glumped all the normal sorry litle bunch of petty malefactors called to account for recent naughtiness. To Leonard, although he did not mention this. Solicitors who bend towards the criminal fraternity base loyalty on intake, and Leonard's business had always been, and obviously would always be, more valued than Freddie's. Freddie was born to be small-time.

Inspector Rosher quite enjoyed the first part of his day. He invariably did enjoy the court, where he was, of course, a well-known figure. Today there were pressmen to be dealt with, shoving forward as Freddie was hurried up the steps and into the grey, handsome building, latest sorry character in a line stretching back to when they were bundled back down these steps to be hanged for stealing a fourpenny loaf, or bustled away (for a twopenny one) to a day or two stinking in the stocks, all covered in flung ordure. There was the time of waiting in the bare corridor, grimly silent for two reasons: one, because it plays upon the subject's nerves; and two, because he had nothing to say.

Then there was his brief appearance in the box, when he asked for permission to remand Freddie in custody, pending further enquiries. Mr Golightly, looking down over his half-moon spectacles from the bench, asked if Mr Marks had any objection. Mr Marks had none, he said. What else could he do? Permission was granted.

And then there was a pleasant drive to the big city gaol, wherein Freddie would be pent until his trial, coming out once weekly for a further appearance in court, a further remand; until he confessed like a man or something turned up to nail him good. If and when he decided to parrot, Rosher would drop everything and toddle over. No other way to arrange the matter; what with striking warders and general undermanning coming at a time of high criminal activity, the prison system teeters on the edge of chaos. It's all very awkward; but prison remand cells are kept relatively free. They have to be.

So Freddie was delivered to the big city, Mr Marks following now in his own car because leaving it in town would have meant coming all the way back to fetch it or paying out money to have it driven home, and paying out money was a thing Mr Marks hated to do, even though he'd clap it on to his bill. He always clapped little things like that on anyway, right down to paperclips, looking upon them as perks. The more you did for yourself, the bigger the perk.

He arrived ten minutes after the police car, being by
nature a circumspect driver; in time to stand by while
Rosher completed the formalities attending the handing
over of live flesh for incarceration, and to wish good-
morning to the two detectives as they left. Freddie's right
to private conference with his solicitor being undisputed,
when he was in his cell they were left alone together.

In the course of a shortish conversation, Mr Marks said:
'I've been in contact with Mr Figgis. Mr Figgis agrees with
me, it's best that you say nothing about the—er—other
matter. Certainly not at this stage.'

'Figgis?' said Freddie. 'You've been on to Figgis?'

'Well, naturally.' Mr Marks's plump smile never
became oily, exactly. But by God, he could be bland. 'Mr
Figgis, as you will appreciate, feels keen interest in
your—welfare. He *and* his friends.'

By the time he said this, the two officers had been
locked through the two enormous steel gates that must be
negotiated, unless buddies on the outside help you over
the wall. The boot of the car had been looked into, just in
case some enterprising character tucked himself in with
the spare wheel, and they had driven away through streets
as dejected and browbeaten as is fitting within the vicinity
of a prison. It all adds to the ambience.

What a lovely day it was. Getting well up through the
morning now, of course. Soon it would be lunch-time;
and still the sun shone out delightedly, as if it had just
mastered the knack. Very little was said in the car as it
purred through that long, dreary area of decrepit shops
and screaming hoardings connected to the city centre;
where it turned along an almost equally squalid road
leading at last to suburbs of better housing, giving way in
turn to raw estates of identical semis destined, given
time—and not too much of that—to make slums in their
own right. Nobody living in them would notice, so long as
it didn't affect the telly. Not until they were well into the

lovely countryside beyond did either of them speak. Since Rosher's outburst en route to collect Freddie from London, verbal traffic between them had been minimal.

There is a good little teashop facing the green in the good village called Thornton Wavers. Rosher it was who said gruffly: 'Fancy a cuppa?'

'We'll be at my place in five minutes,' Boggis answered, in a tone that matched nicely. 'I was thinking we could tap the wife. I've got nothing urgent on, thought I might take a couple of hours off. Have a bit of grub, get cleaned up.' He added, with heavy irony: '*If* you've no objection.'

'Hmmph,' said Rosher. 'Mm. No—you might as well. I'll take the car back.'

'Right,' the sergeant said; and after a moment: 'You're welcome to a cup of instant.'

It was, as he said, five minutes of easy driving from here to Boggis's place, which was a very pleasant cottage set in a tree-leafy lane that ran off from the main road. Sudden acquisition of this cottage lay behind the sergeant's request for transfer from the city. It was left to his wife by her Uncle Ferdie when he dropped in his tracks like a stone, filled with sloe gin on the night of the day when he uncorked last year's bottling. Unhappily, the intervillage bus came along in a hurry to be home, and you can't see much in that unlit lane at night. As the coroner said, Uncle Ferdie should never have been lying there.

It really was a home worth transferring for, especially when until now you have lived since marriage in a police house amid city din and diesel fumes from the bus station next door. They had worked on it, so that the thatched roof nestled snug as a coating of honey. The windows, plain in Uncle's day, had been carefully divided into small diamond panes with cunning plastic strip disguised as lead, and they had chipped a lot of the plaster from walls and ceilings inside to expose the original beams.

The garden was long, narrow and bright with flowers.
Altogether, a nice little house to live in. Rosher and
Boggis trod along the front path at exactly the time when
Charlie Palkin left Leonard's flat and slammed himself
into his car.

Charlie had rung Leonard from a public booth soon after
9 o'clock. No real likelihood that his own phone was
tapped, or Leonard's either; but your wary bent,
especially when actively engaged, prefer not to tinkle
back and forth. Operators do listen in, lines do get
crossed. Even speaking from a booth, Charlie revealed no
more than he had to. He merely said: 'I think we'll have
to get together. We've hit a snag.'

'Uh-huh,' said Leonard. The guarded speech told him
all he needed to know. 'Better come round. Give it an
hour, I'll put out the buzz.' Solid pro. No questions, no
expostulation. No panic.

Soon after 10 o'clock, then, Charlie drove into the
cavernous underground garage serving the high-rise block
and mounted in a plush and purring lift. James
(Horsehead) Rumblelow was here already, sitting in one
of Leonard's Swedish chairs. So was Bernie Stephens,
sitting in another. And Leonard himself, of couse. He'd
answered the chiming door.

He said, when he had ushered Charlie fairly in: 'What's
up, then?'

'The old geezer,' said Charlie. 'Sir Roland bloody Goyt.
He snuffed it.'

'Snuffed it?'

'Fell down dead, the silly old sod.'

'How do you mean, fell down dead?'

So Charlie told it all. He spoke of his connecting with
the gardener and touched briefly upon the means used to
persuade that man to get him into the house. He told it
all: how he disarmed the alarm system; how he visited the

cellar and came face to face with Sir Roland as he
emerged. He told of how he carried the old man up and
left him in his own bed, and the other men listened in
silence. Except Horsehead, who tended to breath through
his mouth owing to mashed sinuses.

When he finished, Leonard spoke. 'Foggen hooray.
Didn't you hear the old twat coming?'

'How could I hear him?' Charlie snapped. He'd had a
bad night. Let no man criticize. 'The foggen carpet's six
inches thick.'

'You could've heard him breaving,' said Horsehead;
who knew it was possible, having been nobbled that way
once himself. How'd you know I was there? he asked the
copper, hauled out from behind a chimneystack. Heard
you breathing, the copper replied.

'Don't talk foggen stupid,' said Charlie. He was getting
that glare in his eye. 'How could I hear him breathing, he
was miles a-fucking-way.'

'They did me,' Horsehead said. He, too, was beginning
to bridle.

'Cool it, cool it.' Leonard cut in. 'Nobody's blaming
you, Charlie. You did right, shoving him back in his
uncle. Cocked it all up a bit, though, ain't it?' Uncle.
Uncle Ned. Cockney rhyming slang for bed. No cockney,
Leonard, but he worked the Smoke for a while, time of
the Kray brothers.

Bernie spoke. 'What's the set-up in the cellar?'

'Like Ernie said it was. I didn't touch nothing, but if
everything works we wouldn't have had no trouble.
Course, I don't know what's under the floor. Only what
Horsehead says Ernie said.'

'We was sharing this cell,' said Horsehead, 'and he says
to me—'

'For Christ's sake,' Leonard snapped. 'We know all
that.'

'Yeah. Well,' said Horsehead, gone belligerent because

he didn't like being snapped at.

'What you reckon to do, then, Leonard?' asked Bernie.

'Hang about, hang about. Haven't had time to think yet, have I? Anybody want a drink?'

'Bit early for me,' said Charlie.

'And me,' said Bernie.

'I'll have one,' said Horsehead. It was never too early for Horsehead since he gave up training. Not that he ever did much of that in the days when he was known to all-in wrestling devotees as the Manhattan Masher. He was always the one who scowled and snarled and put up two fingers. And lost. That's why he gave it up—it hurt, having to lose all the time to a big poove called Beautiful Beau Benjamin, four times a week all over the country. So one night he mauled the Beau, just to show he could have done it all along, and retired to become a burglar.

'Help yourself,' Leonard said. 'Wonder if it's on the wireless? Switch on while you're there, Horse.'

Horsehead, on his way to the drinks, switched on. Shapely from the bedroom came Leonard's new room-mate, this one brunette. She wore the ubiquitous short nightie, brought with her in case of fire and donned just now when she got out of bed. All eyes but Leonard's clicked in their sockets. The salient areas of brunettes show through very clearly. She lisped—Leonard loved a lisp, it made him feel very randy and protective: 'Did thumbody thay dwinkieth?'

'Sod off,' said Leonard. 'I'm thinking.'

'Thod you, darling,' she said, and flounced out. He had a knack, did Leonard, when he wasn't pinning them down, of making pretty girls flounce. He said now to Charlie, as the radio tongued out a toupéed disc jockey fifty years too old for his fatuous patter: 'This gardener geezer, this wotsname—'

'Hardcastle,' said Charlie.

'Yeah, that's him. Was he keen? I mean—did he fall easy?'

'Dead easy,' Charlie told him. 'I was surprised, really. Course, he's there on the old fake ref lark, and I had to point out we could soon get a coupla little bits of bait to swear him back inside, but he didn't really put up no argument. I said we'd cut him in for half a grand.'

'Uh-huh.' It didn't matter to Leonard how much the man was in for, he probably wouldn't get it. 'You don't reckon he's a plant for somebody else?'

'Well—he wouldn't hardly have let me in if he was, would he? He's shit-scared, I can tell you that.'

Bernie spoke up. 'He might have done.'

'Might have done what?'

'Let you in, so he didn't blow that he belongs to somebody. Might have got on the blower. They might be moving in fast, knowing we're on to it.'

'They'll get a shock if they do. The old get's dead.'

'Do you mind?' Leonard said. 'I'm trying to think. And one's enough, Horse. I don't want you half pissed when I come to a decision.'

'What decision?' Horsehead asked, and managed a sly second slurp from bottle to glass.

'I don't know yet, do I, for Christ's sake? I haven't come to one. That's what I keep saying—I'm trying to think.'

'I reckon we'd better scrub it,' said Bernie Stephens.

With a hee-hee-hee the radio disc jockey had just handed over to a newsreader. It gave him one minute to adjust his slipping hair. The new, mellifluous voice wafted through trouble between Israel and Jordan, China and America, Russia and Poland, Catholic and Protestant still blowing each other's kneecaps off in holy Ireland, and all the African nations simultaneously. It then said:

'The death is announced today from his home, Notley House, of Sir Roland Goyt, the armaments millionaire,

said to be one of the world's richest men. Sir Roland, who
was 87, was found in his bed this morning by his housekeeper. He had been ailing for many years and his death
was from heart failure, apparently in his sleep.'

Followed a bit about his springing to the public eye
when an attempt was made last year to hijack that truck
packed with his cupidity. When this finished and the
demented disc jockey cackled back with effusive thanks to
the other man and a plea to the housewife that if she
would only hang on he would supply her later with a
recipe for onion flan, Leonard switched off.

He said: 'You did well, Charlie. You did very well. Died
in his sleep.'

'Yeah,' said Charlie. 'Well, that was the idea, wasn't
it?'

'You did well,' Leonard repeated. 'Now—let me think.'

Sergeant Boggis used his key to open the door, wherein he
had set a small stained-glass window under a shiny
lacquered brass-type coach-lamp, worked from a switch
inside, and guaranteed to conform to BSI standards. He
preceded Inspector Rosher through the door, seeing no
particular reason why he should step aside. Rosher,
black hat between fur-backed hands, stood in the bright
beam-ceilinged hall.

Boggis called: 'It's only me, Ros.'

'About time,' came a female voice from inner regions.
It had a peevish tone. 'I'm surprised you bothered to
come home at all.' Out from the kitchen—Rosher could
see it was the kitchen through the opening door—stepped
a young woman at the plumply attractive stage coming
just before she says to heck with it all and abandons
herself to cream cakes as compensation for marital
disillusion. She stopped short when she saw Rosher, one
hand rising automatically to remove the patterned
headsquare worn against dust. 'Oh,' she said.

'This,' Sergeant Boggis told her, 'is Mr Rosher. My
wife. Rosalyn.'

Rosher wore his brown beam, backed up by his telephone voice. 'How do you do, Mrs Boggis? A great
pleasure, I'm sure.'

'How do you do.' Released from the headsquare her
hair showed blonde, but not quite down to the roots. 'I've
heard a lot about you.' Mainly, that you are a stupid old
bastard who ought to be in a zoo. Bust down for being a
sex maniac.

'I've got a few hours off,' her husband was saying. 'We
were passing, Mr Rosher's dropping me off. Thought we
might click for a cup of coffee before he goes.'

'Oh—yes. Yes—of course.' Mrs Boggis's own social
manner was settling in now, white-toothed where
Rosher's was brown. 'Only dried milk, I'm afraid, can't
think what's happened to the milkman.'

'That will do admirably.' The brown teeth glimmered
dully.

A rub-up with Harpic, she thought, or a biological
detergent might do something for them. I wonder if
you're hairy all over?

'I'll just go up and get a clean shirt,' Boggis said, and
he turned aside to mount the stairs.

'Just look at those flowers!' said Mrs Boggis, in a tut-tut
tone. Rosher looked, at daffodils and irises set in a brown,
fat-bellied pot on a low table. Nothing much wrong with
them that he could see. One daffodil browning a little,
that's all. But she advanced, picked up the vase, said
beaming: 'Won't you come through, Mr Rosher?' and led
the way into her kitchen.

Uncle Ferdie would never have recognized it. He left it
in a right old shambles, concrete-floored, stone-sinked,
two cracked windows and the big pantry at the back filled
with his bottles of sloe gin and those wines made from
whatever God puts into the country having the latent

ability to ferment, and so help the countryman to forget it
all for awhile. There was even a little still in the attic;
which Boggis dismantled and kept very quiet about. He
didn't want the police nosing around.

Now, the room gleamed with new paint, Formica,
rubber-tiled flooring glued in on rest-days, and the
various labour-saving gadgets that diverted a lot of his
salary into the ready palm of the hire-purchase people
and settled on to his wife her crown of boredom. No
reason, really, why she shouldn't have got a job; but what
for? They had no children needing bicycles for Christmas,
there was no demand upon her. And you can sink into a
rut. She worked when they lived in the city, but there's
nothing to do out this way if you don't pack eggs or bark
at sheep.

'Do sit down, Mr Rosher,' she said, wondering if he
really was a sex maniac. 'I've only got instant, I'm afraid
we're quite out of Brazilian.'

'Thank you, thank you,' said Rosher. 'Jolly little place
you have here.' He thought: You're all right now, but I'd
bet you'll go the way the wife went. Fat as a pregnant sow.
He sat himself carefully on a foolish but bright little metal
and plastic chair at the formica-topped table. Yellow and
white the colour scheme, with touches of blue. It looked
very well.

'We've worked at it, of course,' she said. The kettle
must have been already boiling, she had spooned coffee
powder into a cup and was filling it. 'Sugar?'

'It repays it,' said Rosher, still with his brownstone
teeth out in the open air. 'Charming. Thank you. Two.'
And when she brought the coffee, together with digestive
biscuits on a pretty plate: 'Thank you. Most kind.'

He engulfed a biscuit. Reminded, his belly sang out
that it was a long time since last feeding. Summoning
juices, it gargled the message. Rosher coughed to cover it
and lifted the silly little cup, smallest banana of his right

hand outstretched. Cups like that go with liqueurs sipped after dinner. In the morning, in the kitchen, a man needs a sizeable mug with a handle he can get a grip on. Quite honestly, little bits of bone china and such do not go with policemen at all, except such as are destined for high rank and somewhere during early off-duty time gather the sort of wife who embarks them on a long course of training and upward-spurring. Behind every successful man stands a nagging woman. Rosher found the cup tilting slightly. He pinched his fingers to grip, and the handle came off. Body and hot coffee fell in his lap. 'Bother,' he said, very mildly. But he had to struggle, to keep his teeth on display.

'Oh, dear, dear, dear,' she said.

Rosher said, with steam rising from his lap: 'I'm afraid I've broken your nice cup.'

'It doesn't matter, it's only a cup.' And sod it, I'll never match it. Should have known better, what you need is a tin can. 'Better sponge it—it shouldn't stain.'

She turned to the sink as Rosher rose, very warm but rapidly chilling about the genitals. Reaching for a sponge she turned the hot tap on; too far. The jet hit the flower bowl which she had placed in the sink, and bounced. 'Erf,' she said, and jerked backward.

Now Rosher was advancing, a bit preoccupied, because a man who has owned as long as he had a durable blue serge suit does not relish sudden stains upon it right where it looks like uncouth ejaculation or a failure in toilet training. Bump he went, into the nicely ample buttocks that jerked towards him; and to keep his balance, to keep hers, his hands went out around her. He felt them dint into her breasts.

Now: there are psychologists who maintain that no action takes place purely by accident, that subliminal thought shapes it; and without doubt, women with sex on their minds will often suddenly bend when by their so doing a following well-bulled man will be brought into contact at the genital area. Similarly, a man so tackled by a fancied woman will often go straight for the breasts.

But what boots it to explore subliminal motives? Body contact was made, a souped-up boomps-a-daisy, and hands went to mammalia. They came away quickly, the lady giving a gasp—and that, you may think, is significant. Without it on the mind there wouldn't have been time—but not quickly enough to be missed by a husband coming in at the door, saying: 'Ros, where's my—? Oh. Here—what the bloody hell's going on?'

He had a right to ask. His wife was jerking forward, away from Rosher and his clutching hands; and the ape-man's parts seemed to be steaming.

Back to the big city. In his elegant apartment Leonard had been pacing his wall-to-wall carpet, deep in thought while his henchmen sat back in the Swedish chairs, waiting. It was very quiet up here, and very pleasant with the spring sun beaming in through the windows. Peaceful. Only the girl in the back room seethed, for-gotten by the men, who were now resigning themselves to calling the job off. Grave complications had set in.

But not Leonard, that man of rare tenacity. Too much offered here, the once-in-a-lifetime tickle; and Leonard was not so well breeched as he preferred people to think. This flat—his women—a flamboyant lifestyle—they all cost money.

Well, he made money, sometimes a lot of it; but somehow, it all went. This job was to set him on Soft Street for life, in a warm climate beyond extradition laws. If Ronald Biggs could do it, so could he; and with more time than Biggsy had, he'd got it all set up. The false papers, the plane fare paid—he'd invested in the job. And another thing: pride. A man has his pride; and these buggers would spread the word about if he backed away.

So he paced, and thought deeply; and said at last: 'They'll be burying him, then.'

'Well—yeah,' said Charlie. 'They usually do, don't they?'

'Not my mum,' said Horsehead. 'We had her cremated. They plant a little tree in the garden.' He blew his nose, visibly affected.

Leonard ignored him, as did everybody else. 'The wireless said heart failure, he was under the doctor. No post-mortem or nothing, then, is there? Just sign the certificate and call in the undertaker.'

'We had the Co-op,' said Horsehead. 'Shared the divvy stamps out among the family. It seemed the fairest way. You can't just give in, can you? You have to go on living.' His uncle said that, laying a hand upon his shoulder as he sat apart at the ham and pickle tea, weeping. He'd loved his mother, who brought him up alone after his father decamped with a blonde social worker, met when he was in Dartmoor.

'It's been done, mate,' Charlie said.

'What has?' said Leonard.

'Posing as the undertaker. Somebody did it in London, few weeks back.'

'So?' Leonard, too, remembered the newspaper report. It's what gave him the idea. 'Got away with it, didn't they?' A little miffed that Charlie should have followed his thinking so easily.

'That's true. That's true.' Charlie put his nail-file away. Work with edgy alarm systems demands delicacy of touch. Alarms specialists and skilled safe manipulators commonly have well-tended hands.

Bernie, too, had been using his file. He spoke now, eyes still ranging among the cuticles. 'Chancy, though. Very crafty, the Old Bill. They may have give out natural causes to keep it all dark.'

'Keep what dark?'

'I dunno. But you can't trust 'em.'

'They wouldn't keep it dark if they thought he'd been done, would they? There wouldn't be any point.'

'That's true. That's true,' said Charlie.

'Well, then. Who'll be going to the funeral?'

'I don't know, do I?'

'What about your friend Sandcastle?'

'Hardcastle.'

'That's him, yeah. He ought to be able to find out. Put the armlock on him, eh? Point out what happened to the old get and tell him he's an accomplice.'

'I didden half put the armlock on bleeding Beau Benji,' said Horsehead. 'Bust it in two places, above the elbow. He's meat-humping now, Smithfield way. One's shorter than the other, they tell me.'

'I could try him,' Charlie said. He, too, was reluctant to see all that loot go, probably to others not so easily deterred. He, too, had a lifestyle calling for constant inflow; but horses were what lapped his money up. 'No harm in trying him.'

'I don't know,' said Bernie Stephens. 'It's dicey. Looks very dicey to me. I don't believe in sodding about with the dead.'

Leonard rounded on him. 'You want in or out? Only say now! We can always get somebody else.'

'I didn't say I wanted out, did I? So long as it's feasible.' Bernie was another who had waited long for big tickle, and at least emotionally had invested in it. He was going to have a greyhound stable of his very own. He'd already been to view it. Nice little place, Wolverhampton way.

'All right, then,' said Leonard. 'What about you, Horse?'

'Yeah, I'll have a drop of scotch,' said Horsehead, coming back from a golden memory of how the Beau yelled when his arm went snap, snap.

'For Chrissake,' Leonard said. 'You want in or out?'

'I'm in, ain't I? You wooden know nothing about it if it hadn't been for me.'

'All right, Charlie,' said Leonard. 'Why don't you nip over there? See what you can do.'

'Why not? Don't want to give no other bugger a chance to get in first, do we?'

So away went Charlie, at just the time when Boggis led Rosher up his primula-bordered path. He was well on the way to the town by the time Rosher relinquished Mrs Boggis's tits as if they glowed white-hot, and the sergeant said what the bloody hell's going on here.

'What the bloody hell's going on here?' said Sergeant Boggis.

'Ah,' said Inspector Rosher. A last wisp of steam came up from his sociable area.

'I was just—getting the sponge,' said Mrs Boggis.

'Sponge?' Nasty tone. All policemen are quick to suspicion, it's an occupational disease. And he knew about Rosher. Well—he knew the lurid exaggerations that were side-mouthed about Rosher.

'To rub his trousers,' she said.

'His what?'

Now she flared; but she'd turned pink; so more than likely she did have what lay under on her mind. The young girl blushing is no innocent, inside. 'Oh—don't be daft, Reg.'

'Daft? I come in here—'

'Rrrrmph,' said Rosher. 'Don't be bloody stupid.'

'Stupid, am I? You—'

The wife lifted up her voice. 'Mr Rosher spilled his coffee in his lap, his handle came off. Look—there's the cup, on the table.' Rosher had plucked it off his trousers and put it there.

'So he gets up and grabs your—'

'That'll do.' It came from Rosher in the authentic Old

Blubbergut bark. 'That's quite enough.'

'Oh, I'm glad it's enough.' Boggis could bark, too. 'I thought you might have further plans.'

'Oh—shut up, you bloody fool.' Pink and angry, his wife turned to the sink; lifted the fat-bellied flower bowl and banged it down so hard it cracked. 'There—now look what you've made me do.'

'Use your loaf,' Rosher barked. 'I'm not likely to get up and—with you around.'

Why not? Wouldn't be the first time, would it?'

The implication hit Rosher full in the face. The publican's wife, the busting down, all the traumatic humiliation. No good saying, as prisoners do when they come up against job problems after release, that once a man has paid for his lapses the matter should be forgotten. People don't forget, they see forever the leopard with all his spots. But Rosher by deep instinct backed by years of training was a fighter. Now he felt his fists bunch—those mighty fists with which he automatically clobbered out of sudden pain in his boxing days. His ring-clever mind knew without needing to think exactly the point on Boggis's jutting jaw where impact on the nerve centre would stretch him slumbering on the rubber tiling.

But it wouldn't do, it wouldn't do. He forced his fingers away from his palms; reached into his pocket and brought forth the dreaded handkerchief. Raised it and blew a blast that shocked right through anger and jealousy. Boggis and his wife jumped visibly and stood looking at him. The very daffodils shook in the cracked pot. He wiped up; stowed the handkerchief; coughed, and with a forefinger scratched the little tonsure on the crown of his head. Then he moved to pick up the black hat from where he had put it on the table. 'I think I'd better be going,' he said.

'Yes. Yes.' Boggis's tone came quieter now. Truth to

tell, he was beginning too late to wonder if he had overreacted, if the sudden, surprising uprage of jealousy had carried him too far. But he, too, was a fighter, very much in the Rosher mould. His fists, too, had clenched. 'Yes. Yes, I think you had.'

'I know the way out,' said Rosher; and so rattled was he by the happening that he clapped on his black hat in the presence of a lady in her own home before he tramped away.

Mrs Boggis turned on her husband before the front door-slam died away. 'You bloody fool,' she said.

She was right, of course; but the wife of a man like Boggis does well to button the lip, especially when a voice in his gut is telling him she might be right. Rosher would never have stood mildly for such an attack from his own fat wife. 'Oh, am I?' said Boggis. 'Am I? How many other people grab a quick handful? Bloody good job I was here, ain't it?'

'How dare you?' she cried. 'How *dare* you!' And she felt, deep in her anger, the fierce sexual pleasure that infuses a woman when she is about to embark upon an emotional scene with a husband made jealous by a man who must have found her worthy, or he wouldn't have grabbed her by the tits.

Oh, aye—and a mighty fine scene they made of it.

CHAPTER 11

When Charlie Palkin reached the town he left his car among many in the car-park attached to the big supermarket which has shouldered its way past the screams of conservationists to cuckoo among the old town centre shops, and would take the whole of the market square over if it could. Some day it might, when it has butchered all the remaining little shopkeepers. Rampant greed has its way, eventually.

Charlie was no conservationist, except in the guarding of his own assets. To him, the park presented a very handy convenience. As, indeed, it did to many patrons of the town centre hostelries, short-cutting home at turning-out time. Not very bright, to drive out now to Notley House and leave the car in the woods, as he did before. From here, he'd walk. A pretty fair step; but he'd walked before, he knew how to do it.

He approached that useful hut from the lane once more, and lurked in it for perhaps half an hour before the gardener appeared. Things were going nicely. Charlie had quite expected a longer lurk, perhaps even until knocking-off time, when he would have to come upon Ollie out of a bush again; but here the man was, trowel in one hand, box of bedding plants in the other, about to bend over at a dug bed nearby. No more than a low whistle and a beckoning finger needed to bid him come hither.

Ollie came into the shed and shut the door quickly, saying: 'What—what do you want?'

'Just a quiet word, Ollie boy,' Charlie said, exuding good humour. 'Nothing to get worked up about.'

'He's dead,' said Ollie. 'The old man—he's dead.'

'Well, I know that, don't I? I was there, wasn't I?'

'You—you—killed . . .' This was the fear that had been added to fear.

'Now, now, now, don't let's jump to no conclusions. It's all down to natural causes, ain't it?'

'I don't want—' said Ollie.

'Hang about, hang about,' Charlie said. 'All we want's a little bit of help.'

'Help?'

'Information. Like—who's in the house?'

'I don't want—' Ollie said again. 'I don't want nothing to do with it.'

'Ah, but you got no choice, really, have you? Let me
put you in the picture. There I am, see, coming round by
the banisters—'

'I can't hang about in here.'

'Yes, you can, for a couple of minutes. Pretend to be
sharpening a shovel or something.' Charlie sketched in,
very neatly, the salient details relating to the old man's
sudden demise. And he ended: 'So whatever happens to
me happens to you. Doesn't it? You let me in—you're
down for accessory.'

He would never have tried this line on a pro, of course.
Any pro knowing anything at all of law would have told
him to get stuffed. But Ollie was not a pro, he was merely
a sexual deviant once incarcerated among his betters. So
Charlie watched the man's rising panic-fear, and added:
'And there's the false refs caper still outstanding, ain't
there? And I'm authorized to up you from five hundred
quid to seven-fifty.'

'What—what do you want to know?' said Ollie.

'That's my boy. Who's arriving for the funeral?'

'Only his nephew. He's here already, in the house.'

'Nobody else?'

'He's the only relative, Mrs Rummidge says.'

That was handy. 'When are they digging him in?'

'Tomorrow.'

'That's a bit rapid. Still, I suppose there's not much
point in keeping him in the fridge. Who's doing the job?'

'Job?'

'Undertaker. Who's handling it?'

'Oh. Sugden and Fawse.'

'Local, are they?'

'Yes. Chalmers Street.'

'What time?'

'Half past eleven.'

'Uh-huh. And there's only one mourner?'

'Yes. Well—Mrs Rummidge will be going.'

'Are you invited?'

'I'll have to go. Yes.'

'Uh-huh.' Charlie let his good intent beam in his smile again. 'You're a good lad, Ollie. Got it all at your fingertips, eh?'

'Mrs Rummidge came to see me.'

'Good. Very good. Wouldn't be surprised if we up you to a grand. Buy your own sweetie shop, eh? Get 'em wholesale. Sod off, now. If we need you some more I'll be in touch.'

Ollie went back into the sunshine; bent again to his work. No sign of life in the house, standing with blinds drawn at this time of grief. Charlie slipped again through the loose boarding and walked all the way back to town, pausing only once to pee behind a hedge. Dead easy. Within the hour he was back with Leonard and the boys.

That was a troubled hour for Rosher, and even more so for Boggis. The former drove to the police station, and left again after lunching off sausage, chips, two tinned tomatoes and a mug of that fearsome tea, to bring in for questioning one Stuart Nichols, who foolishly took off a glove in a dark house at 3 o'clock in the morning to help himself to a buckshee shot of whisky and left beautiful dabs on the decanter. All through the trip out and the drive back, and through the questioning after—indeed, all through the rest of the day—he seethed with indignation against the sheer stupidity of the situation so suddenly arisen. Not that he'd ever kidded himself a dog given a bad name is not vulnerable to sudden hanging; but sod it—he hadn't had an erection for Christ knew how long, and didn't even want one.

The Boggises both had an even harder time. The trouble with quarrelling, between people who stifle the abrasions normal to monogamous marriage, is that repression leads deeper into resentment and so on to simmering hostility. When the bust-up arrives—look out.

One of the paradoxes in feminine argument is that the woman who least enjoys her husband complains most bitterly because he is never home. In the married life of a detective, it's a chief bone of contention. She chewed upon it now.

'It's part of the job,' he yelled. 'You knew it when you married me.'

'That was a bloody bad day,' she yelled back. 'If I'd known what I know now . . .'

And so on. You know how it is. In the end he grabbed his hat and stormed out, leaving her to bang pots about in her gleaming kitchen.

He went to the station. His car being parked still on the forecourt, where he left it this morning, he caught the bus from the end of the lane. One minute later in his storming out and he'd have had three hours to wait for the next. Or a long walk, which might have cooled him down. As it was, he arrived with the rage still upon him. Sergeant Barney Dancey, that good man, looked out from his little glass booth as he entered and said: 'Hi, Reg.' Boggis stalked by without answering. 'What's up with him?' Barney wondered to himself, and bent to his work again. Bad-tempered CID men are no riveting novelty.

It chanced—malicious little Fates enjoy a giggle, sometimes—that Inspector Rosher, in his black hat, stepped from his office to embark on the picking up of Stuart Nichols just as his sergeant came stalking along the clacky-floored passage.

Boggis said—silly, but a man with a cannonball head, enraged, has to push it: 'When you're in my house, keep your hands off my wife.'

Rosher, too, had a cannonball head. Bristling, he barked: 'Don't be bloody stupid,' and went on his way. The sergeant clacked on to the CID room. Round the L-bend at the end of the corridor, where filing cabinets

stand overflowed from the Records Room, WPC Alma
Toddy closed the metal drawer quietly and moved off,
tittering inside. The old ram was at it again.

They put it to the vote. Not that the risks involved were so
great as to boggle the eyes, they had all taken part in
ventures more obviously dangerous; but the shape of this
enterprise had changed very quickly, and sensible
criminals mislike the wham-bam-thanks-ma'am
operation. They prefer leisurely planning, and orderly
procedure.

On the other hand: as Leonard said: 'Look—this kind
of tickle don't crop up every day, does it? It's once in a
lifetime, ain't it?'

'I still reckon,' said Bernie, a nervous man at heart and
one who carried a rabbit's foot when he operated. Turned
away, once, from a diamond-stuffed safe in Hatton
Garden because he'd left it behind. 'I still reckon we
ought to wait until *after* the funeral. When the house is
empty. We can take our time then, operate in peace.'

'We don't know if it's going to *be* empty, do we? This
nephew geezer might be moving in, if it's left to him in
the will.'

'They have to prove the will first, don't they?'

'I dunno. Do they, Charlie?'

'Why ask me?' said Charlie. 'Nobody never left me
nothing.'

'I got my mum's cameo brooch,' said Horsehead, 'and
eighty nicker out of the Post Office savings. Only the
bastards took the cameo brooch because it fell orf the
back of a lorry.' Nobody took any notice of him.

'Give Alfie Marks a bell,' said Charlie. 'He'll be able to
tell you.'

'It don't really signify,' Leonard said. 'We all know
what the problem is. If Ernie told Horsehead, he might
have told somebody else.' Or Horsehead might, was the

shared thought, he being a right twat. But no one said it aloud. Horsehead, umbrage taken, was also very destructive. This was no time for broken bones. 'If we hang about, we're liable to get in there and find the bloody lot gone.'

'That's true,' said Charlie. 'That's very true.' Others having the matter under review might well see opportunity offered. And he'd already put the alarm system out of action. The place was all set up. If they didn't press on—at some time, somebody would tumble that the alarms had been fiddled with. Or—worse—other operators would reap the benefit of his setting up. Delay would add to the dangers: of approaching the house at all, and of finding nothing left in it when they did.

'It's too quick,' said Bernie. 'That's my only worry. I mean—I'm the one who's got to get the bleeding safe open.'

'Well—you reckoned it was a bit of bleeding cake.' As Bernie had, when Horsehead passed on what Ernie Parvis said was the make and pattern of the safe.

'Well—yeah. That's no problem,' Bernie said. 'I just don't like all the rushing about, that's all.'

'All right,' said Leonard. 'We'll put it to the vote. But: anybody opts out, they have to understand that them in favour reserves the right to call on replacements.'

This is no way to conduct a plebiscite, it smacks of coercion. Not that anybody seemed to notice. Certainly, nobody demurred; because the one thing above all that your bent cannot do is turn his back on such tickle knowing that he is letting in some other bastard—whom, if he is a specialist, he will certainly know—to a life in the sun, laughing at him from the beach if it comes off and just a spell of porridge if it doesn't; while he himself must grind on with much face lost, a routine tickle here, a tickle there, and porridge anyway from time to time, until old age and bitter regret marry him to the dust. So there was not a single nay, nor even an abstention.

Leonard said, after the count: 'Good. That's all right, then. We all know what we're going to do, right? We'd better get off, then. Hang on, I'll get the shooters. And listen—don't load 'em, until I give the word. Right?'

They set off at once in Leonard's car. Charlie and Bernie did not even pack an overnight bag. Time, now, was of the essence. They called in briefly at Bernie's flat to collect his little bag of tools, and they stopped at Woolworth's to buy two clotheslines. These small halts apart, they made the town in one uninterrupted run; and here they cruised about, looking at Chalmers Street and its surroundings, noting the things they needed to know. Three pairs of professional eyes, summing matters up; and one pair looking at everything with interest, having enjoyed the ride.

At length, Charlie said: 'What do you think, then?'

'I think we go ahead,' Leonard replied. 'Looks simple enough, don't it?'

'Right,' said Charlie. 'Put us down in the town square, we'll make our way up on foot.'

So Leonard set them down in the market square and drove away with Horsehead. A lovely walk it was, to the big house, the weather holding up remarkably for so early in the year. Charlie enjoyed it thoroughly, already feeling that tickle in the belly, that heightening of *joie de vivre* that comes when a man sets forth to serve his vocation; but nervous Bernie said, as they crossed a giggling stream by an aged lichen-crusty packhorse bridge, the scene a veritable jewel in England's crown:

'I don't like shooters. Bloody things are dangerous.'

'One of these days,' Charlie told him, 'you're going to wake up with an ulcer. You're not even going to load it, I don't suppose any of us will. It's a deterrent, that's all. Look at the beautiful country and think of which piece you're going to buy.'

No rush. They even sat and rested here and there, Charlie snuffing the air and recommending it enthusiastically to Bernie, who really preferred a nice night-club and the scent of a hostess, preferably blonde. A little manipulation with one of his instruments, and they were inside and waiting when Ollie Hardcastle came home to his cottage immediately after work—he had given up his evening pint, becoming ever more certain that everybody was looking at him.

When he came into his parlour—in old tied cottages a parlour is still a parlour, and remains so until some bloody fool and his wife buy it, and tear down walls to make it open-plan—sat the terrible Palkin, lounged at ease in his chair; and another man, identity not known, sitting less easily on the over-stuffed sofa.

'Hallo, Ollie boy,' said Charlie, cheerful and well-intentioned as ever. 'Surprise, surprise.'

'What—what—' Ollie said. 'How—how did you get in?'

Charlie indicated Bernie. 'A little waggle with a buttonhook. My friend never travels without 'em.' He did not name his friend.

'What—what do you want?' He's going to be sick, Bernie thought.

'A little bit more help.'

'I—don't want . . . I can't . . . I've done all I can . . .'

'All we want is for you to do it all over again. We need to get into the house.' Which we could do as easily as we got in here. But as Leonard says, you have to come in with us. The deeper you're involved, the less you're going to shoot off your mouth. Certainly you're coming now we've let you know we're here. No leaving you to panic and go rushing off to find a blower. And you had to know we're here—you might have come mooching in for a game of Monopoly with the lady.

'I—I can't. Mrs Rummidge . . .'

'Don't worry about it, she won't even see you. If you've

got a bit of bread and cheese handy, we'll talk about it while we shift 'em. I'm bloody starving.'

No great hurry, you see. The only reason they came tonight was because it would be much easier to get in than if they left it until the morning. Also, of course, it gave Bernie all the time in the world to operate, and that's always insurance against snags, even when a specialist such as he reckons to open the safe like Heinz Beanz. The stuff could all be packed and ready. And people are better dealt with at leisure than if you have to shove a hurried boot in the door and grab them before they scream, in the broad light of day.

Ollie, taking the request literally, produced bread and a hunk of cheese. Charlie made a hearty supper, having suggested that the basic be augmented with mustard pickle and tea; but Bernie ate little, and Ollie nothing at all. Then they watched television for awhile, again at Charlie's suggestion. Around 8 o'clock they all stepped out into the dark garden, Bernie carrying the washing-lines. That Charlie was a very persuasive man. By the time he produced stocking-masks from his pocket and tossed one to Ollie, saying: 'Here—better put this on, just in case,' he was meeting no resistance. 'You should always wear one of them,' he said through nylon when Ollie had donned it. 'It suits you, it really does.'

There was plenty of shrubbery between the cottage and the house. They used it. Ollie, with the key, took longer to open the door than Bernie would have needed using one of his little manipulators. When Charlie, to still the rattling, had guided the shaking hand and they stood inside the conservatory, he produced his shooter. Webley .38, ex-army. Old-fashioned, but very effective. Bit bulky, that's the only trouble, worn with today's more tightly tailored suits.

Ollie said, and when he gasped his opened mouth and squashed nose under the nylon made him look like a rough sketch by Hieronymus Bosch: 'No—no—not—'

'Don't worry, don't worry,' Charlie soothed. His stocking was worn with a certain élan. Experience counts, in everything. 'Nobody's going to get shot.' He didn't say so, but it wasn't even loaded. Who wants a bloody great gun going off after dark in an isolated country house? And they weren't here to shoot people, anyway. 'All right.' He gestured with the barrel. 'Let's have the other door open.'

Now they were in the passage that led to the hall. They moved quietly along it, Ollie in the middle in case he got ideas about running. A strip of light showed from under the door to that drawing-room where Rosher stood when he called—and where two solidly ranking officers had stood since, ostensibly come for young Evie's clothing. They found nothing else—and Charlie gestured with his back hand, to stop them. 'Right,' he whispered. 'Hang about. Gimme the rope;' and he crept onward across the hall, thoroughly enjoying himself.

He opened the door, very quietly. A thin-looking man with a black, forbidding moustache sat in one of the armchairs, reading and looking surprisingly like one of the balder characters in a Charles Dickens novel.

Charlie said, quietly but firmly: 'If you don't do nothing silly you won't get hurt.'

The man's head jerked up, eyes shocked and black, mouth a round hole. And then he lurched to his feet, clutched his chest, said: 'Er—er—urgh,' and—you wouldn't believe it, would you?—fell flat on his face.

'Oh, Jesus Christ,' said Charlie. 'Oh no. Oh, Jesus Christ!' He said it not in panic, but with deep exasperation. Sod it, it was becoming a regular occurrence.

He bent over the fallen man and turned him, to bring him on to his back. Inserted his cotton-gloved hand—every sensible villain wears gloves—between clean

white shirt and chest. Not a flicker. Hopefully, he felt for
a pulse in the wrist. Nothing. He even took a glove off, for
better contact. Nothing. 'Oh, fucking hell,' he said. 'My
fucking luck.' And he stood up, replacing the glove.

No man can think of everything, of course; but it might
be well for the bent who creep about in other people's
houses, appearing just like that in stocking-mask with
gun, to consider the phenomenal rise of late in the
incidence of heart conditions among middle-aged men.
This one was middle-aged, if you count it as continuing
up to the late fifties. He lay on his back, a corpse with a
bald head and a mean-looking moustache. He'd been
reading Gibbon's *Decline and Fall*, taken out from a
bookshelf.

'Sod it,' Charlie muttered. 'What did the silly bugger
do that for? It's going to upset Bernie.' Bernie the
superstitious, edgy already. He might well decide that the
entire project was jinxed, and panic accordingly. Panic
does not assist in the efficient opening of safes; and the
baby-stuffer was gibbering already. Two of 'em, taking it
on from each other all night—very dodgy. Much—all—
depended now on Bernie.

I'll sit him in a chair, he thought. Tie him up like we
planned, it'll keep him upright.

He lifted the body, reaching around it under the arms.
The head lolled and nodded as he dragged it to an easy
chair, the one with its back to the door, and sat it there.
As he unravelled the washing-line a voice whispered from
the doorway. 'All right?'

It was Bernie, speaking through his stocking. 'Yeah,'
said Charlie. 'No problem. I'm just tying him up.' He
addressed the corpse. 'Sit nice and steady, chum,
nobody's going to hurt you.' He added, as Bernie showed
signs of advancing: 'Don't leave our mate out there on his
tod—stay with him.'

Ollie needed to be watched over, in case in his panic he

broke and rushed away, or crept off while they were looking in the other direction. Bernie knew this as well as Charlie; he'd only come to make sure Charlie was coming back, it seemed so long since he went. 'Yeah—yeah,' he whispered, and tiptoed away. All he'd seen of the man was the bald top of his head.

With the man tied neatly and looking, apart from glassy eyes, very lifelike, Charlie came out from the drawing-room, closed the door softly and recrossed the hall. 'All right, then,' he whispered to Ollie. 'So where's the old lady hang out?' Which speech would not have given pleasure to Mrs Rummidge, still no more than middle-aged. Accepting, once again, that the condition persists into the late fifties.

'Upstairs,' Ollie said.

'Lead on,' said Charlie.

Mrs Rummidge had her housekeeper's suite of large sitting-room, decent-sized bedroom and poky converted bathroom-cum-lavatory on the first floor, close by the master suite where Sir Roland lay still, all washed and shaved and made decent for burying. Easy for the creeping men to select the right door, even without Ollie's nod. The telltale strip of light shone from beneath it.

Inside, Mrs Rummidge was trapping her hair into those metal curlers, having just washed and coloured it up a bit for the funeral. Her new black hung over the back of the easy-chair beside a fire lit against the chill of a spring night, she having just tried it on. Her feet were in her old slippers, her corset rested beside the black, her teeth were in the bathroom and she stood at the miror on the wall above the fireplace, warming her belly gently while she messed about with her wet hair. Into the mirror came a reflection that surprised her: the room door opening, and a head looking like a turnip crowned with a quite County cloth cap poking itself in.

She might well have screamed there and then; but a

lady caught straggle-haired and half-curlered, in locknit
knickers and OS bra with her corset over there and her
teeth smiling widely in the bathroom, thinks first on these
things. Nobody would have heard her anyway, the
nephew downstairs gone beyond it and neighbours a long
way off, but it was the priority factor that made her spin,
one hand flying to her mouth partly because she was
startled and partly to hide its lack of furniture, while she
said:

'What—who are—get out! Get out!'

'It's all right, darling,' Charlie said, advancing with his
gun. Bernie peered in briefly and vanished again, staying
on the landing with Ollie. 'It's all right, dear.'

'Get out! Get out!' she said.

'Nobody's going to hurt you,' said Charlie, soothingly
like a vet about to castrate a cat, 'so long as you don't do
nothing silly.' He didn't want this one dropping dead.
Not that she looked as though she would. Very strongly
built, tits like the great, rock-solid puddings they serve in
HM prisons at Christmas, which whittle down to one
small portion per reveller, with custard.

'Get out, get out, get out,' she said; and bolted for the
bathroom, slamming the door and locking it behind her
before he could head her off. He rattled at the knob.
'Don't be silly, darling,' he said. 'Nobody's going to hurt
you.'

'What do you want?' she cried. No furry edges to it, no
lisping. She had whipped her teeth in already. Didn't
hang about. 'Who are you? What do you want?'

'Nothing of yours, dear,' said Charlie. 'We don't intend
you no harm at all, we're only after a few bits and pieces.'

She lifted up her voice. 'Help!' she shrieked. 'Police!
Help! Help! Police!'

'Shut your row, you silly old cow,' said Charlie.

Bernie appeared again. 'What's up? What's up?' he
said.

'She's locked herself in the bog.'

'Sod that.'

'Help! Police!' shrieked Mrs Rummidge.

'Can't you get her out?' said Bernie, in a hoarse whisper. Why he bothered to whisper now is anybody's guess.

'Don't be bloody stupid,' Charlie snarled. 'If I could I bleeding would, wouldn't I?'

'Police!' went Mrs Rummidge. 'Help! Police!'

'We'd better scarper.' This was Bernie, a new nervous tic visible even under his stocking. 'They'll hear her.' He didn't say who. What did it matter? Anyone with a finger to dial 999 would do.

Now Ollie was here, babbling through the cacophony of Mrs Rummidge's screaming. 'What are you doing? What are you doing to her?'

'She's locked herself in,' Charlie said; and added: 'The window—somebody'll have to get in through the window, shut her up.' Before she got out of it, and buggered matters completely.

'It hasn't got a window,' Ollie gibbered. 'An extractor fan—it's got a big extractor fan, that's all.' Part of his job was to cure dripping taps, unblock U-bends, things like that.

Charlie snarled at Bernie. 'Pick it.'

'Scarper—let's—'

'Pick it!'

Bernie produced a little something, not from the toolbag but out of his pocket. He carried useful and innocuous articles where they were handy. Mark of ingrained professionalism that his hands, shaking until they approached the keyhole, steadied immediately when he touched it. In a few seconds only, during which time Mrs Rummidge stopped screaming, he'd clicked the lock back. This is when Charlie loaded his gun, while he waited. Not with any kind of murderous intent, but because it seemed a good thing to do. If this old bird was going to show fight, to be armed with an empty gun would rob gestures of significance. And Ollie was showing signs of utter terror, he'd be easier to control knowing the gun was loaded. Knowing it was empty, he might well chance trying to scarper; which would mean a fight, at least, and somebody probably hurt.

Bernie, job done, stood aside, having no wish to be the man who opened the door. And Ollie stood well back to avoid being seen by Mrs Rummidge. Charlie it was who pushed the door open, cautiously and with gun extended. You never know what a big-busted woman gone silent intends to do to the first man in. A tin of Harpic can inflict a grievous wound, brought down sharp end first.

The lady was standing on the lavatory seat. People retreating normally seek corners, and the lavatory stood in the corner farthest from the door. She was not fighting. Her goggling eyes and open mouth, her stance upon the toilet suggested that she had leaped up there out of the reach of a raging mouse.

Charlie spoke without his soothing tone. 'You silly old bag, get down.'

'Hoo—hoo—hoo,' she said.

'Come on—down.' He crossed and grabbed a wrist. Jerked her down. She stood with her avoirdupois quivering, saying: 'Hoo—hoo—hoo.'

Charlie called. 'Oy! Henry!' Bernie would know the call was for him. On a job, you don't give real names.

Sure enough, he appeared. Charlie said: 'Get the rope.'

When the rope appeared, the one not used to bind the nephew, he sat Mrs Rummidge down on the lavatory seat and bound her there, passing the cord behind the pipe leading up to the old-fashioned cistern. Partitioned off in the 'thirties, this cubicle, and never inspected since. They wouldn't allow it nowadays. 'Now, my old sweetheart,' he said, 'sit there nice and quiet. If you holler we'll have to

gag you.' A glance had told him that so long as she was in
here a bit of shrieking wouldn't do much harm. No
window at all; the way out for steam, as Ollie had said,
via a big extractor fan set high up. And the walls, in these
old houses, are very thick. In Victorian days, when Pater
beat the screaming children or sent Mater into hysterics,
he didn't want the world to know.

Having her nicely trussed and giving out only low
moans, he picked up the key prodded on to the floor by
Bernie's manipulations and went out into the sitting-
room, locking the door behind him.

Bernie said: 'It's going to be bloody chilly in there,
nothing on.'

'So she shouldn't have gone in,' snapped Charlie. Even
his nerves were stretching. 'She'll be all right, we'll sling a
blanket over her later.' It made sense, to leave her there.
Better not to have Ollie seen, better that she should
glimpse them only rather than sit here studying them,
their voices and possible giveaway habits. And they'd
have to keep their masks on all night; because he meant
them to stay in here, where there was a fire and some
measure of comfort. If she was in here, Ollie would have
to be elsewhere; and this would mean keeping an eye on
two people in different places. Not really feasible, there
was work to be done. 'All right, then, let's get cracking.
Ollie—you come with me. In front, that's right. And
don't forget there's a popgun behind you.'

At the head of the handsome stairs, Bernie peeled off
to go down. Charlie directed Ollie on, into the master
bedroom where Sir Roland lay, looking remarkably well,
considering. 'Now we'll just lift him out,' Charlie said,
'and lay him on the bed.'

'I can't—I can't—' said Ollie.

'Oh yes you can, son. I'll let you have the light end.
Grab hold of his feet.'

So they lifted Sir Roland out, leaving the coffin nice

and empty for when Bernie came up to repack it; privately, because the less Ollie knew about the loot, the opening cellar and the job in general, the better. Charlie shepherded the quaking gardener back to the comfortable living-room; where he said:

'All right, china—sit down, make yourself comfy. You can smoke if you want to, only chuck the fag ends into the fire. Keep your gloves on, but you can take your mask off. She can't see you, don't worry.'

Bernie, by now, was in the cellar; still nervous but settling nicely, as the good pro does once his own part in the action begins. He counted the wall blocks and found the right one, just where Ernie said it would be. A beautiful piece of engineering. It simply eased out until it stood proud from the wall, by about three inches; when it triggered, so that this great, thick slab of paving stone tilted up in absolute silence, carefully counter-balanced. Leading down into the strong-room beneath were wooden steps.

Bernie descended. Not very big, the stone-walled, stone-floored vault. Just about large enough to hold a couple of medium-sized men. But beautifully done, with the safe door showing in the wall to the left. He produced a small piece of emery cloth from his toolbag to sensitize his fingers, looking around as he rubbed and murmuring: 'Bloody lovely.'

Well-merited tribute to a highly talented gunsmith from one of Sir Roland's factories, who vanished almost immediately after building it before he even received, never mind spent, the small fortune he'd been promised. 'Bloody lovely,' said Bernie; and he flexed his own clever fingers, bent his head to listen for the tumblers' click. 'You'd have thought he'd have got a better safe.'

Detective-Sergeant Boggis had no real need to, but he worked late again. That is: when he found nothing left to do at the station he made a tour of pubs and clubs where villains were known to foregather; not seeking anything but staying away from home, as men often do when the blaze of anger dies down to sullen resentment. Serve the bitch right if he never went back at all. When he finally arrived in his house, Mrs Boggis had gone to bed. He found bread, cheese, two kinds of pickle, butter and a cup on the kitchen table, together with a note.

It said: 'Didn't cook. Supper on table.'

Very terse. No crosses at the bottom, no signature even. Sod you, too, he thought.

He ate some supper and had a shower. In pyjamas and dressing-gown he then went into the living-room. Switched the television on and watched for ten minutes before he said bloody rubbish and switched it off again. After which, he locked up and went to bed.

She was lying turned away from him, and he knew bloody well she wasn't asleep. But he said nothing. He took off his dressing-gown and climbed into bed, keeping carefully to his own half; turned the light off and settled down to hours of fuming, knowing that she was doing it, too.

So they lay, backs turned upon each other all night, the only physical contact happening when one, dozing, stirred a little and bumped their bums together. Nothing in all this to make Rosher more dear.

CHAPTER 12

Detective-Inspector Rosher had nothing pressing in his book; wherefore, he was frying a leisurely egg in his kitchen next morning when the telephone rang. Sod it, he said, because an egg whipped off half-done and fried up again after takes on a rubbery texture; and moving the

pan to one side he went out into the hall, where the
telephone yelled.

It was WPC Maisie Stokes, on duty at the station
switchboard. 'Good morning, Mr Rosher,' she chirruped,
wondering if she'd called the old ram off the nest. It
seemed he was at it again. 'The City's just been on. Your
man Lugge, he's asked to see you.'

'Ah,' said Rosher. 'Good. Good.'

'Hang on a minute, the Chief wants a word.'

A moment, and the Chief Constable spoke. 'Mr
Rosher—good morning. Lugge has asked to see you.'

'So I understand, sir.' *What was the strange smell of
burning?*

'Confession, do you think?'

'I imagine so, yes.'

'If you've nothing urgent to see to, perhaps you'll get
over there straightaway.'

'Will you hang on just a moment, sir?' Rosher hurried
back to the kitchen. His tea-towel with the cornflower
motif, dumped too close to the gas flame when he
answered the phone, was smouldering sulkily. He doused
it in the sink. Went back to the hall. 'Sorry about that,
sir. Yes—I'll be away in a few minutes.'

'Don't bother to come down,' the Chief said. 'One of
the cars can pick you up. See if you can find out what he
did with the handbag.'

'I will.' *Of course I bloody will. He'll tell me,
presumably.*

'Good. Splendid. Carry on, then. Call in and see me
when you get back, will you?'

'Uh-huh.'

'Good. Splendid. Well done.' Away went the Chief,
and WPC Maisie Stokes pulled his plug out.

Inspector Rosher went back once again to the kitchen.
He dumped the tea-towel into the bucket kept filled with
detergent-water under the sink—*drop your smalls in,*

leave them to soak, and in a day or two they wash with minimal rubbing—and put his egg back on. He had it eaten between bread and washed down with tea fit for the tin guts of robots by the time a squad car arrived, manned by a boy who looked too young to drive, never mind be a policeman. So many of them looked like that to Rosher, these days.

He was, actually, a very nice lad, having a mother who worried about him, a father who thought he'd have done better working, as he himself did, for the Department of Health and Social Security, and a fiancée who wondered how she could introduce into their trafficking without causing him to ponder some of the tricks taught to her by previous fiancés, one a French perfume salesman.

Rosher knew none of these interesting facts, and neither did he want to. He took one look at the pink cheeks and bright eyes and elected to ride in the back. Sit beside the little sods and unless you nip it quick in the bud, they prattle.

They made fair time to the city gaol, and were checked and double-checked in. The inspector found Freddie sitting on his bunk in his remand cell, all on his own and not confessing, after all.

Poor Freddie had spent the night as he spent every night: tossing and turning, all in a sweat. Tormented by two fears: one, that he would be convicted of a murder he did not commit; and the other, that in attempting to weaken the case against him he would call upon himself terrible retribution. Because he knew the police: they'd hang on, watch Leonard, nobble him in the act; and that would bring Leonard himself, and those other hard men, inside. And he, Freddie, would not be liberated just like that, they'd have him as accessory, at least. And for withholding information and—oh, they were bastards, they'd cook a string of charges up. No proof, once he told this copper, that he'd turned Queen's Evidence, even.

But Leonard would know.

They might—probably would—all wind up in the same nick. He might find himself with Leonard—or Horsehead—or that bastard Charlie Palkin—sharing the same cell. Stranger things happen, in this day of overcrowding.

Oh—they'd have no doubt who grassed. Even his own solicitor was back-handed by them. He should have gone for somebody on the Legal Aid list. They didn't know he'd got a bit of money tucked away.

Through the small hours he fretted, coming at last again to decision. He'd tell it all. Murder meant life. Well—not literally, he'd be paroled in, maybe, ten years. But ten years—of queers and horrors . . . whereas he couldn't get more than a couple, as accessory to robbery. He might get nothing, if he cooperated. Which is the police euphemism for grassing.

So when the early screw rattled on the door with his keys and cried wakey wakey, he asked to see Rosher.

But: between the breakfast he couldn't eat and the inspector's arrival, his tremulous pendulum swung again. Think what can happen in two years. A man can die of it. Horribly. And if he doesn't—they can have a reception committee waiting at the very gate, or they can strike out of the blue any time after; and able to operate without needing to be on the blind side of the screws. A man known to have grassed is never free again from fear. Not even if he scarpers. There are underground connections all over the place, and nobody loves the grass. Not even the policeman.

On the other hand: people in tricky positions who keep the lip buttoned are sometimes rewarded. Looked after. If Leonard and his friends were *his* friends—well—at least they'd keep the queers off his back.

So when the horrible ape-man arrived in his cell, saying: 'Well, my lad?', Freddie said: 'I didn't do it, Mr Rosher. I swear I didn't do it.'

That wasn't what Rosher expected to hear. 'That's not what I expected to hear,' he barked. 'I thought you were going to be sensible.'

'I didn't do her,' said Freddie. 'Honest to God, I didn't do her.'

'Did you bring me all the way over to tell me that? It won't do, lad, will it? It just won't do. What do you say, Constable?'

The pink-cheeked young man come in as witness started, finding himself addressed almost for the first time since he picked the old bugger up. Sod for the women, they reckoned, had a go yesterday at Boggis's wife. 'Ah—no,' he said. 'No, it won't do.'

'I think we'd better have another little chat.' The great gorilla stood there in his black hat, drawing back prehensile lips to show horrible brown eye-teeth.

'I swear I didn't do it,' Freddie said.

Half an hour later Rosher left; disappointed, but not downhearted. It had happened to him often enough before, the call from a subject on remand suggesting confession, turning into stubborn reaffirmation of innocence. Freddie might change the tune later in the week, when he came again before the magistrate to be remanded in custody for a further seven days; or later, as the nerve-racked weeks went by until he could be tried.

Before he left, the inspector said: 'We've got you to rights, you know, son. Make it easy for yourself. What did you do with her handbag?'

'I never touched her handbag. I swear it.'

'Doing a lot of swearing, lad, aren't you? Never get to heaven that way.' And I notice you didn't ask for your solicitor.

It felt good, to the young policeman, to be driving away from gaol. The young who are not neanderthally moronic tend to find upsetting the sheer ugliness of the environment, the casual insensitivity of officers who do

not seem aware of the terrible system they serve, the evil
in prisoners not eradicated by imprisonment but simply
compressed into here, out of society's sight. But
policemen who survive to Rosher's age have seen it all too
often, and know the side-effects of criminal activity too
well, for any such reaction. Rosher, in any case, was never
over-sensitive; even in his rookie days he saw black, and
he saw white. If the bastard's bent, clap the bastard
inside. Armoured in this philosophy, he sat in the back of
the car and thought his thoughts, which veered between
Boggis, Boggis's wife and various villains likely to be
responsible for the various jobs in his book; until they
approached the town. By which time, Boggis was about
to make his call.

Boggis was in a foul temper. The row with his wife blew
up again this morning; gone beyond Rosher now, raging
over mutual resentments built up through seven years of
not very compatible marriage, kept private until now but
brooded over all night, relative molehills building into
mountains through the sleepless hours.

After breakfast—and she burned the bloody bacon—as
he donned his hat she said: 'And what time do you reckon
to come back?'

'How the hell do I know?' She knew as well as he did, it
depended upon what happened during the day.

'I shouldn't bank on finding me here.' She stood by the
table, very stiff.

'Oh, I won't,' he said. 'Don't worry about that. Give my
regards to your old bitch of a mother.' And he slammed
the door going out.

Now he sat black-browed in the front seat of a squad
car beside a driver who left him alone, having heard the
story going the rounds alleging that the man's wife was
touched up yesterday by Old Blubbergut, wearing his
goat-beard again. Probably exaggerated, although they

reckoned—he hadn't been here when they bust the old lecher down—that when he got randy, Rosher grabbed for the nearest tit.

They were on the way to bring in, if he was at home, the little man who, a whisperer confided, broke into the Co-op supermarket last Friday and crept out with a load of goodies and a wad of dividend stamps, together with the wee books to stick them in. Funny thing to do, but then many small-time operators are a bit peculiar. Choice of purloinable materials is conditioned, quite often, by early environment. This little fellow's mother was a glutton for Co-op stamps.

There sat Boggis, then, glowering through the windscreen as the driver manipulated the car through the town centre, which calls for a little less in the way of iron nerve since they built the bypass to take the juggernauts away; thinking not of his work but of his wife. That's where she'd go, of course. To her mother's. Sit down, dear. Don't cry, have a nice hot cup of tea. Tell Mother—what's the bastard done now?

Well—she needn't bloody well bother to come back. He'd change the bloody locks. He was well shot of the whole bloody lot of 'em. He wouldn't be surprised if the bloody milkman had her every morning, standing up on the bloody step. The cow.

And they'd better bloody well keep him away from Rosher. Not that he could say anything about it at the station without laying himself open to looking a right berk. But they'd better keep him away from Rosher, that's all.

The first thing he noticed about the hearse, as it came towards them along the street called Bondgate, was: it seemed to have only one man in it. A second man, presumably, was driving the big limousine following along behind; but usually, two men sit in the front of a hearse. Here was only one. So Boggis raised his glowering eyes; with no great interest but simply because he was a policeman, and policemen are trained to notice anything out of kink.

His eyes focused suddenly. He said: 'That's Leonard bloody Figgis.'

'Who is?' said the driver. For the record, here is his name. PC Walter (Wally) Wargrave. Quick man with a jest. Too bloody quick, many said.

'In the hearse.'

'What did he die of?'

'Driving the bloody hearse—that's Leonard Figgis. And that's—' the limousine was going by now—'that's Horsehead Rumblelow. Pull in—pull in. Over there—turn round.'

Over there was a courtyard, fronting a pub. 'You're the boss,' said PC Wargrave; and he signalled a right turn; turned the car round while Sergeant Boggis unhitched the microphone and asked the station to come in. When the radio squawked, he said:

'Sergeant Boggis. Car Eff-Four. Eff-Four. I've just spotted two villains. One's a big boy from my old patch. In the city. Leonard Figgis. The other one's called James Rumblelow. They're dressed up as undertakers.'

'As what?'

'Undertakers. Black top-hats, all the gear. Figgis is driving a hearse. Rumblelow's in a funeral limousine. Stand by—I'm following.'

'Roger,' said the radio crisply. No dickering.

PC Wargrave knew his business, he did not need telling that discretion is necessary when you set out after a subject, probably no mug, in a distinctively marked police car. But he said nothing, this was the kind of job he enjoyed. Several cars between all the way, he followed the black vehicles to the very edge of town; where they turned on to the winding road that dwindles to the lane that runs past the house of the late Sir Roland Goyt.

Boggis reached for the microphone just as a voice tinned out of the radio. 'Car Eff-Four. Car Eff-Four. Come in, car Eff-Four. Over.'

'Car Eff-Four,' said Boggis. 'Over.'

'Where are you? Over.' It sounded like a canned version of Inspector (Bongo) Fowler.

Boggis gave the location. He said: 'It'll be a bit trickier, keeping out of sight from here.'

'You could have stopped 'em in town,' said Inspector (Bongo) Fowler. 'As I understood it, you were going to. Over.'

Boggis hadn't said he was going to apprehend, the bloke who passed the message on must have jumped to the conclusion. Reasonable enough conclusion, of course, two known villains making like undertakers away to a funeral are acting in a manner sufficiently bizarre to warrant their apprehension on suss. But Boggis—oh, he shared so many character traits with Rosher. A throwback, really, to Rosher's generation, last of the true chauvinist pig line—believed always in finding out what the buggers are up to, catching them red-handed if possible. He had no idea what size of enterprise they were engaged on; but Leonard was well capable of organizing a big one, he didn't go around at night upending cigarette machines.

And another thing: go roaring after them with siren screaming and you can start up a chase—highly dangerous in crowded streets. Innocent bystander damaged—maybe killed—and right up the creek goes the copper who instituted the matter. So Boggis replied stiffly.

'Impossible. Somebody could have been killed.'

The car was proceeding along that road which dwindles, Constable Wargrave holding it back, so that the two funeral vehicles were out of sight on the far side of the first of many bends. He said: 'There's only three

buildings along here. One's a pub, one's a retired admiral
and the other's Sir Roland Goyt. And he's dead.' He
didn't need to say it, but he could have added: And they
reckon the house is full of loot.

Boggis had never been along this lane; but a man who
spends his shifts patrolling in a squad car knows his areas
inch by inch. The sergeant said into his microphone:
'Hold on a minute;' and to PC Wargrave: 'Where does
the road go to?'

'Comes out on the bypass. About three miles, no side
turnings. Straight on for the city.'

'Are you there, car Eff—what's the bloody number?'
the radio said.

Sergeant Boggis spoke into the mike. 'It's my bet
they're on the way to Sir Roland Goyt's house—he's about
due to be buried. I suggest a general call to all cars in the
area. The lane comes out on to the bypass. One car in
from there could block it, one in from this end would
bottle 'em. But you'll have to move it.'

'How many of 'em did you say there are?' The
implication was quite plain: how many cars and bodies do
you need, then, to deal with just two little men? Great big
boys like you.

'Two, so far as we know. But they may be meeting
others. I saw an old mate of one of 'em, in town the other
day.' Charlie Palkin. Wouldn't mind betting the bearded
geezer he was with was something to do with Sir Roland
Goyt.

'All right,' said Inspector (Bongo) Fowler. 'Stay with
'em, I'll put the buzz around. Over and out.'

Almost immediately the voice of the duty operator
came, calling all cars in the vicinity. One of which
contained Rosher and his young driver. They were, in
fact, nearly level with the bypass end of the lane when the
little voice spoke, and they'd heard what went before
because there is no block between radios in police cars.

Neither needed to say a word. The young man simply
swung the wheel, and into the lane they went. All Rosher
had to do was grunt, and reach for the microphone.

CHAPTER 13

Leonard was up this morning early, quitting the soft arms
of his brunette—he was getting a bit tired of them,
actually—a long time before he usually did. Poring over
the map bought yesterday in town, he had set well into his
mind the salient features of Chalmers Street, home of
Sugden and Fawse, Funeral Directors, and the layout of
all the streets about. He knew from his reconnaissance the
route to Notley House and the one-way system he would
have to negotiate on parallel roads, to get back. But best
get there early, for an unobtrusive check. You can find a
system altered overnight, a road closed or even gone
altogether. Things change fast nowadays.

He was not idle, after he got home yesterday afternoon.
There was hire to be arranged of a very common
production-line van with a real bowl of soup under the
bonnet, from a man who specialized—and still does—in
such things. Not that need for a racing getaway was
envisioned or likely, but a man in a van filled with trinkets
rides easier knowing he has power under his foot.

Then there was the matter of a call to London,
arranging for the urgent delivery of decent black. There
is a bent theatrical costumier who makes more from his
sideline than he ever does from amateur pantomimes.
He'll rig you out as whatever you fancy, and keep your
measurements on file. Aye, and do it all in a hurry,
delivering to here and picking up from there. For a price.
You'd hire cheaper locally; but of course, you'd have to
appear in person, for measurement and so on. The lads

find this London man very useful. The man who shops him will direct to himself considerable wrath.

A certain amount of time was necessarily devoted to the briefing of James Rumblelow, into whose well-hammered head things sank slowly, if at all. Leonard would have preferred to leave him behind, taking in his place a more nimble-brained herbert hired for the night; but Horsehead might take umbrage, and whisky to go with it. An umbraged Horsehead drinking might very well sob to sympathetic ears; and to introduce an outsider now could be equally risky. So with commendable patience he explained to the big man just what he had to do. Over and over again. Made Horsehead repeat it all by rote, to make sure he had the hang of it. Told him to lay off the liquor this night.

When Horsehead was gone, instructed in exactly which corner of the city square he would be picked up from at 8.30 in the morning, there was personal packing to be done; because when he had returned that fast van to the stable, after a quick run to Nottingham where a man stood ready to receive the goods and pass them on, he wanted to call in here only briefly, to collect his case. And away with Charlie—out on the first plane tomorrow. The Nottingham man would play it straight, and follow on later. He was Leonard's brother. What Horsehead and Bernie intended to do he wasn't sure and didn't much care, so long as he was gone beyond extradition. They'd get their share—and Horsehead, going mad with it, would probably gaol them both. Hard luck, those two men.

Packing finished, it was time to meet the London man at the arranged point, and to stow bundles into the hired van, which he left for the night in the underground garage. In the flat again he explained to the brunette that he'd packed because business would be taking him away for a few days. She asked no questions, he was not her first man of dubious habit.

He watched with her a little television and ate a meal
off a tray, all brought in from the Indian takeaway. Then
there was the business of having sex on the rug, because it
suddenly came over him, as it commonly does when the
mounting adrenalin-charge brings a man fully alive. As
he lay on his back with her sitting astride, propped
against his knees—she liked it that way, and since
(although she didn't know it) this was their last joust, he
felt disposed to pleasure her nicely—the telephone rang.
Three times, and then it stopped. Charlie, ringing with
the signal announcing that they were in, and all well at
his end. She didn't even hear it. Her head was thrown
back and she was going hoo-hoo-hoo.

He slept reasonably well, disengaging from her
snuggled warmth at 7 o'clock. Showered, shaved and easy
in the bowel, he picked up Horsehead at the time
arranged and pointed the tiger-engined van at the town.
Both wore working overalls.

Rush hour is a good time to arrive, if you need to check
routes so that you know which are liable to morning snarl-
ups, best avoided if you wish to go somewhere in a hurry.
Also, a vehicle is never so anonymous as when it is in a
maelstrom. They checked the undertaker's, finding it all
they remembered and more—private alley alongside, and
at the back a covered yard with only waste ground behind
a defunct factory fronting it; in which yard, yesterday's
peeping said, a hearse and two limousines were kept.
Perfect. Seeing this had provided the final spur. Press on,
it was made for the job.

They went next to the road leading to the lane leading
to the house. Didn't enter the lane, just made sure they
knew exactly where it was and how to get to it. And then
they drove around, Leonard assessing the areas, until
10.30; which he considered a fair time to arrive back at
the undertaker's premises.

Actually, there was a hole in his planning here. What if the undertaker had had an earlier funeral, and driven straight on to pick up Sir Roland from wherever this took place? He didn't think of that, even now. Well, of course, he'd had to plan in a hurry; and it made no difference, as it happened. Sir Roland was opening corpse of the day.

At 10.30 they drove up, stopped the car outside the premises of Messrs Sugden and Fawse, and took the chance that had to be taken. Not such a big chance at that, with only a strip of pavement to cross and no pedestrian near. They donned their stocking masks and entered the front parlour, Horsehead carrying the rope. Dark carpet here, and discreet potted greenery about. Even an aspidistra, and a bell above the door that made a sorrowing bong as you entered.

Mr Sugden—who undertook Mr Fawse two years ago; the poor man died, there being no exemption for undertakers—stepped into the hush from a back room. He was dressed for another fun-filled day. He said, richly solemn: 'Good morning, gentlemen.' Then he noticed the masks, and the gun Leonard was levelling, and added: 'What? What? Who—what are you?'

'Back inside, Dad,' said Leonard. 'Move it and you won't get hurt.' He didn't particularly like guns, although he had carried one quite often when it seemed a good idea. Today, certainly, he had reasoned, there'd be no time for argument, and a gun is a powerful persuader. People rarely scream, faced suddenly with a gun. Shocked, they do what they are told. Few look closely, to see if the thing's loaded. His wasn't—his instruction applied to himself. No loading. He wasn't looking for accidents, there was no vicious liking in him for violence.

Mr Sugden almost fell back into the interior room; which was big and bare, apart from several coffins on trestles, and one on the floor close to the door, upon which sat two bald men in mourning eating bacon sandwiches. They looked up, and froze with mouths opened to bite. 'Stay where you are, lads,' Leonard said, 'and don't make a sound.'

No need to instruct Horsehead in this. He moved forward; and sudden confrontation with him in a stocking mask almost outstripped the power of a gun as persuader. In a very short time he had three men neatly bundled, using knots he learned in the navy before his court-martial. He liked knots. They wouldn't get out of this lot. Leonard said: 'Look upstairs.'

Horsehead took out his revolver. Another Webley .38. Soldiers flog them. He didn't know it, but even if you loaded it you couldn't make it fire. Leonard had no intention of entrusting a real shooter to Horsehead, of all people. Too many bangs on the head in his ring days, and more when he was bodyguard to Big Tony Oliphant in the Smoke. It made him unpredictable, especially under stress. So even while he watched television last night, Leonard was not idle. He took the firing-pin out, and said nothing. To have denied the big man outright, when everybody else was to carry a gun, would have called forth umbrage.

Up the stairs he went now, gun extended, and came down soon with a plumpish lady having a slight cast in her right eye; who looked at the trussed Mr Sugden and said viciously: 'Why don't you do something, you old fool?' As if he could, all tied up like that. To say nothing of the guns, and hulking Horsehead.

'Tie her up,' Leonard said. This, presumably, was Mrs Sugden. Unless they lived in sin. Which wasn't likely, it takes a wife to speak like that.

Horsehead moved in again. Respectful as his adored mother taught him always to be towards women, herself especially, he said: 'Sorry, lady. It won't hurt.'

The woman turned her evil ire upon him. 'Get on with it, man, get on with it,' she snapped. He actually said sorry again; but he tied her up good. And she was the first to be gagged—immediately, because that free-range and beady eye might well spot, if it knew about such matters, that the guns were unlimbered. A woman screaming in an undertaker's back room brings neighbours running, if only to see if he's readying the old bat for premature attention at last.

'Right,' said Leonard, when they were all made dumb. 'Watch 'em.' And he went out through the yard where the black vehicles stood and down the wide drive-in alley to the street, leaving Horsehead standing about with his gun.

He drove the van into the yard. No problem, anybody seeing a man in overalls driving a van into an alley takes no notice. Only a few minutes needed, to change into black, retest knots, turn the card hung at the front door to make it say closed; bolt the door, remove car keys from a hook in the back room and lock the door behind them when they stood in the yard, Horsehead holding the bundle of black clothing for Charlie and Bernie.

'Right,' said Leonard. 'You get out and lock the yard gate behind us. Look—there's the key, on the inside of the lock. You move it to the outside.' Better make sure he knows. He's just as likely to lock himself back in, and drop the bloody key down a drainhole. It's like working with a musclebound Stan Laurel.

'Yeah. Right,' said Horsehead, and went to the limousine.

Leonard got into the hearse. Peeled off his mask. Started the engine. Looked in his rear-view mirror and got out again. Went back to the limousine and said through the window:

'You going to drive through the town like that?'

'Like what?' said Horsehead.

'With your bleeding mask on?'

'You didden say take it orf.'

'Oh, for Christ's sake!' The big twat looked odd enough in that hat, without this. Why couldn't he have been somebody else? *Anybody* else. 'Get the fucking thing off.'

No incident, on the way to Sir Roland's house. They drew up solemnly in the drive while Sergeant Boggis, out of sight round the bend behind them, was talking to Inspector Bongo Fowler at the station. Leonard re-donned his mask, came out from the hearse and glanced around. Nobody about. Only Horsehead, putting stress on the seams of his mute's clothing as he ducked out from the limousine carrying the bundle. The house door opened as they approached and Charlie stood there, looking through nylon.

'All right?' said Leonard.

'Yeah—yeah—great,' Charlie said. 'Couple of things have cropped up, that's all.'

Before the small voice of the duty operator had finished battling through static to put out his general call, Detective-Sergeant Boggis was out of the car, decision already made.

He said to PC Wally Wargrave as that man alighted: 'You sure there's only one house down here?'

'Uh-huh. About a hundred yards ahead.'

'Can we get to it through the woods?'

'I've never done it, but—yes, I suppose so.'

'Come on, then.'

'Leave the car here?'

'Well—we can't drive it through the bloody trees, can we?'

'We could go straight in,' PC Wargrave said. 'There's only two of 'em.'

Yet another character trait shared by Rosher and Boggis was this: each took unkindly to the junior rank who implied criticism of his course of action. So the sergeant said, his own version of the Rosher bark in it: 'Let's go.'

PC Wargrave shrugged his shoulders. 'You're the guv'nor.' He followed on into the bushes fringing the road.

In this case, Boggis was right. Inviting calamity, to drive straight in. By now, if this was indeed their target the men would be inside the house. And somebody—the geezer with the beard?—was in there to let them in. Horsehead was dumb enough for anything; but Figgis was a ranking pro, he wouldn't fiddle about on the doorstep waiting for an innocent inmate to answer his ring. That meant accomplices—two? Four? Six? Eight?—who had already taken care of the mourning party.

That probably meant guns. Policemen know as well as any of the bent that a gun is the only effective persuader when you need to keep a body of people—and there could be a dozen mourners, ready-made hostages if necessary—under control and silent while you tie them up, or shepherd them into a cellar. And Figgis had carried guns before, Boggis himself had been one of a team that went out armed for a bank job.

So he was quite right, to do what he did; which was lead on to the edge of the garden, there to wait with his head down, hidden by shrubbery with PC Wargrave beside him, the hearse and limousine standing there by the balustraded steps and the subjects gone into the house. Other cars would be on the way, right now. Wait, then, for reinforcements. If they came in from both ends, even if he had to let the quarry through there was no way for a funeral to turn without finding the lane blocked.

'Keep down, keep down,' he snarled softly as PC Wargrave looked over the top of a dwarf rhododendron; and he settled himself to peer from beneath a variegated holly, supporting himself on his elbows; while Rosher advanced along the lane, travelling fast and as silently as a well-tended internal combustion unit knows how.

★

'All right?' said Leonard.

'Yeah,' Charlie said. 'Yeah—great. Couple of things have cropped up, that's all.'

'What kind of things?' Leonard stepped inside. Horsehead followed. The door closed.

'Well—the bloke who was here for the funeral. Nephew or something. He's—in there.'

'Good. Tied up?'

'Well—no. I had to untie him. I needed the rope for the reporter. He's dead. Only don't tell Bernie.'

'Who's dead?'

'This geezer, this nephew. He keeled over. Just like his uncle.'

'Fucking hell,' said Leonard. 'I don't believe it. It's bloody ridiculous.'

'Yeah, I know,' said Charlie. 'That's what I said.'

'Reporter? What reporter?'

'Young feller. Local rag. I've got him in there. His car's in the garage.' Nasty moment, that was. The car's approach, the young man watched through the stained-glass window as he came on—all the other windows remained shuttered—and rang the bell. When Charlie answered, he said: 'Good morning—sorry to bother you on a day like this. I'm from the *Courier*.' Then his mouth sagged, in the customary fashion when people register a mask and a gun. 'Come in,' Charlie had said. And now he was in the smaller drawing-room. It had shaken Bernie. Charlie had to go himself, to get the car off the drive and under cover.

But Bernie had perked up again, reinspecting the loot which he had packed into the coffin, trotting with it up and down the stairs as he abstracted it from the safe while Charlie remained on guard behind the closed drawing-room door, watching over Ollie more than over Mrs Rummidge, who spent the night quietly enough on her lavatory seat wrapped in the counterpane from her bed.

Bringing Ollie with him, Bernie now came down the stairs from the lady's sitting-room. 'Wait till you see it,' he chortled to Leonard. 'Just you wait. We couldn't get it all in.'

'Where is it?' Leonard asked. His eyes had flicked briefly over Ollie. Big lad, but harmless. Soft as putty, and shit-scared.

'Upstairs. In the old man's bedroom.' Charlie rolled his mask back. 'There's six bloody great paintings still down there, we couldn't get 'em in the box.'

'They'll go in the hearse, propped up. It's got dark windows and curtains. Let's go up, then, eh?'

'This way,' said Charlie. Quite the little host.

Inspector Rosher brought his car closer to the house than Sergeant Boggis brought his. This was partly due to the fact that the house stood towards the end of the long bend from which he approached, so he was nearer to the house gates when they came in sight; and partly because of a difference in tactical theory. Boggis knew that no other copper was here. Rosher knew that Boggis was, probably engaged and needing assistance; so he came on fast.

But: he was too wily a bird to come flapping his wings and croaking. It was obvious that whoever these rogues were, here was where they were perpetrating roguery. Were it not so, he'd have bumped into them in the lane.

So: they must be after big tickle. And villains after big tickle in this day and age commonly go armed. The police do not, except on the rare occasion when arms are issued to deal with a specific situation.

Short of the house gates, then, he said to this driver: 'Stop here. No—don't pull in, block the road.' If they scarpered and came this way, they wouldn't get past. He added as he ducked from the car: 'Go down the road a bit, see if you can find Sergeant Boggis and whoever's with him. Tell him I'm here. If you don't see 'em, come

back and get under cover, back of the house. Get on the
radio first, tell 'em they may be armed.' He went into the
grounds; not through the gates but twenty yards away,
scrambling up the bank and so into the bushes.

Upstairs in his bedroom, Sir Roland lay neatly shrouded
on his bed, looking waxy but more benevolently tranquil
than he ever looked in life. The unlidded coffin stood on
its trestles; and Leonard said: 'Bloody hell!' Horsehead
said: 'Cor!'

Bernie had done a certain amount of triumphant
stage-managing, to produce just this reaction. He had
stacked the gold bars two boxes deep down the middle of
the fine, brass-handled casket; the hinged tops of the
upper tier opened back so that the metal gleamed prettily
under the light, still switched on because of the shuttered
windows. Rare manuscripts—more valuable than
bullion, but gold and a sparkle are what your burgling
bent love to see—were hidden down the sides, helping to
keep upright the old man's collection of smaller-sized
Picassos against the oak walls. Hidden, because on top of
them, mouths opened to show the twinkling, were many
wash-leather bags.

'Bloody hell,' Leonard said again. 'Beautiful.
Beautiful.'

'Wait till you see the tomfoolery,' said Bernie excitedly.
Tomfoolery is jewellery. And who wouldn't be excited?
'Look—look at that bloody diamond. Big as a bloody
cokernut.'

The great Hordern diamond—that's the one, vanished
from Hatton Garden years ago—lay fatly, twickering on
its blue velvet, artfully placed at the head of the coffin.
Not so big as a cokernut, of course, a man can get carried
away. But not far off golf-ball.

'Lovely. Lovely,' said Leonard reverently. Better than
he had expected. He only hoped it wasn't too big for the

organization his brother had lined up. But it wouldn't be, they were multinational. By Christ, he'd done it! This was it—the big, big tickle.

'It's bloody heavy,' Charlie said. 'And we couldn't get it all in.' He indicated more bundles, more canvases tied face to face and standing by. The paintings could not be seen, but this was Sir Roland's medieval stuff. 'And there's still the six pictures I told you about. Downstairs.'

'Right,' said Leonard. Good boy, Charlie—he'd be the brain that said pack it full, having Horsehead in mind. Brain the big man had not, but you couldn't fault him on muscle. And the Boldcastle geezer was a big lad, too. 'We'll get the coffin in first. Horse—you at one end.' A nod at Ollie. 'You give a hand with the other.'

'I—I—' said Ollie.

'Don't fucking argue,' Leonard said. 'I don't want to turn nasty. Let's get the lid on. Charlie—where's this dead geezer?'

That was tactless. Bernie's nose pointed at once, quivering. 'Dead? What geezer? Who's dead?' He looked at Charlie. 'You didn't—you didn't knock him off?' Because the only geezer he could tie the word geezer to was the young geezer from the local rag, watched this morning through a crack in the broom-closet door when he went into it with Ollie, at Charlie's command, while Charlie opened the front door and marched the geezer through the hall at gunpoint. He'd taken the nephew's well-being on trust.

'Nobody's dead,' Charlie snapped. 'Don't be fucking stupid.'

'He said dead.' Bernie, little beads of sweat on his forehead, was working himself up again. Ollie was affected, too. His mouth had opened. 'What did he say about dead for?' Silly, really. Unless Charlie strangled him with his bare hands—extremely unlikely—a shot would have rung through the entire house. But fear and superstition are not a mixture conducive to clear thinking.

Leonard took the hint from Charlie. 'Nobody's dead, don't be a twat. Get changed.' He looked at Ollie. 'Where's your black, china?'

'In the cottage,' Ollie said. Delivered there yesterday by the hire firm, after Mrs Rummidge phoned them to give his measurements. Hire fee to come out of the estate.

'Why didn't you bring it over?'

'Well—I didn't think—' Nor had Charlie. Nor Bernie. 'I can go and get it.'

Not bloody likely. I can see your brain working, you'll take to the woods. 'No—no—get that lid nailed down.' Sod it—when a funeral drives away, everybody being borne along should be in black. But it couldn't be helped—no time to frig about, and this one wasn't to be trusted alone.

Men in a hurry change clothes very quickly; and these men were in a hurry. If Ollie and Horsehead stood outside the general pattern of thinking—one being numb with fear, the other rendered permanently that way by a lifetime of being battered punchy—edginess in the others was enhanced by the possibility of more reporters arriving. In fact, they need not have worried, only the local press had interest in the matter now. Bigger fish than Sir Roland had swum into the fryers of the county and national papers. Last night a duke shot a duchess, catching her knickerless with a stud groom. But the villain on a job, already hypped on adrenalin, tends to overreact to the unexpected happening.

Bernie, more than any, wanted to be out of here and away. He did not believe there was nobody dead in this house, knocked off in some way by Charlie, who must have kept it from him and whispered it into Leonard's ear. If he knocked this one off—maybe he did Sir Roland?

They weren't to be trusted, then, were they? They were doing things he didn't know about, maybe involving him in murder. He'd had a premonition about the job, he'd wanted to pull out.

Well—too late for that and no time to argue now. He laid his harmless and feared shooter on the bed beside Charlie's and took his shoes and socks off. Rolled his trousers well above the knee at just the time when Inspector Rosher, outside, crept forward to close with the house. Before Charlie had knotted his black tie, almost before Horsehead and Ollie between them had the coffin lid nailed down, he stood ready to go, in a black dress that sagged on him because he lacked bosom and width of hip, adjusting Mrs Rummidge's black hat with the pious veil. Well—people familiar with the household would expect to see her there. Somebody had to play female, they couldn't take her in person. So unpredictable, women. She might have gone hysterical, screaming her head off.

Inspector Alfred Stanley Rosher, when he reached the garden-side fringe of the shrubbery, lay under a bush and surveyed the terrain. Nothing moving, the hearse and the limousine standing docile in the drive. He wondered where Sergeant Boggis was. No sign of him.

Well—there shouldn't be. Say what you like about the bone-headed bastard, he knows enough to stay out of sight. Even if he sees me—which he won't have done, up to now—if he's got any sense he won't signal. Probably eyes, behind those shutters.

My guess is that he's in those bushes over there, because we didn't see his car so he'd have come in from that side. Probably with his driver, unless he sent him to cover the back. Which I wouldn't have done—not then. They'll come this way, I'd have wanted two to tackle 'em. Leave the next arrivals to watch the back. So: there should be three of us and the boy. And others on the way.

Thus the thinking of Inspector Rosher, hard little eyes scanning, face—although he didn't know it—grimly simian, the familiar beat of adrenalin in his blood. And it didn't stop there. It went on.

If the bugger hadn't crept close in, he ought to do it. Somebody ought to be there, to panic 'em. Flush 'em away from those cars so whoever else is here by then and tucked in the woods can up and nobble 'em. We don't want a bloody Kojak car chase.

And next into the mind came this thought:

They'll probably give up at once. Kudos to the man who pops up and knocks 'em.

Kudos to him, if it's him.

Sod that. And where was Inspector Rosher? Lying a long way off? Head down under a bush? Well, fancy. Well done, Sergeant Boggis.

If they are armed—more elevated still the eyebrows, if you're lying here while he gets on with it . . .

So: get yourself over there. If he is there—far side of the door—you'll have 'em between you.

There was a kink in this thinking; born, of course, from Old Blubbergut's cordial mislike for sharing any kudos likely to accrue from a case in which he should have starring role; plus antipathy to this particular sergeant, heightened by the incident of yesterday.

So when Sergeant Boggis had his first sight of Rosher as the inspector came from under his bush to cross rapidly a corner of lawn and duck into roses fronting the house wall, it should need no saying that with his similar temperament he reacted in like manner. He thought:

The bastard. This one's mine. The glory-grabbing bastard, the dirty old man. First the wife, and now he wants to make it look as if he did it all while I kept my head down under a hedge.

Bad thinking. Unprofessional. But—well—that's what

an injudicious squeeze will do, when the appendage
squeezed juts from the wife of a man antipathetic.

'Stay here,' said Boggis to PC Wargrave. 'Come in
when you see me challenge. Not before.' And he wriggled
out from his cover; risked a tiptoe dash across the strip of
lawn; fetched up crouched against this side of the hearse.
And Rosher didn't even see him move—he had eased
forward among the rose-bushes to close with the doorway,
and Boggis was hidden from him all the way by the bulk
of the cars.

Nobody chaffed Bernie, nobody asked him for a kiss or
reckoned to fancy him, as men normally do when a man
dons drag. This was no time for joking, this was serious
business with the nerves keyed up tight. As Ollie and
Horsehead finished the fastening of the coffin lid,
Leonard snapped:

'Right. Let's get it down, shove it in first and the loose
stuff around it. Horsehead—get hold of the front. You
and me—' he nodded again at Ollie—'at the back.
Charlie—you and Bernie bring the loose stuff down, leave
it in the hall and go and get them pictures. You sure the
old lady's all right, Charlie? And the other geezers?' This
he added to reassure Bernie. Bernie was definitely
quivering.

'Yeah,' said Charlie, always quick to back up. He'd
worked with Bernie often, he knew the problem. 'The old
lady's on the bog, the others are in the drawing-room. No
trouble.'

'We'll give the Old Bill a bell soon as we get home,'
Leonard said. 'Tell 'em where to find 'em. You can use
one of your funny voices, Bern. Right—let's go. Hup.'

The front end on Horsehead's mighty shoulder, the
back shared between himself and Ollie, Leonard thought
as they carried the heavy coffin down the handsome
stairs: There ought to be four pall-bearers, really, and all

of 'em ought to be in black. Can't be helped—and even if
somebody's watching, we'll be clear now before they can
do more than wonder about it.

Behind him, Charlie and Bernie carried the loose
bundles down. Plate in them, with a glorious Queen
Anne silver teaset and many like baubles. As Horsehead's
enormous free hand reached to open the front door they
put these things down and peeled off in the direction of
the cellar.

Inspector Rosher, crouched behind a Dorothy Perkins
that budded very nicely some four, five yards away, saw
the door open and the entourage come forth. He thought:
Christ—that first bloke's a big bastard. Where's Boggis?
Go for 'em now? No—wait. Could be somebody else
inside. Get 'em when they're loaded and think they're
clear. They'll all be here then—and reinforcements ought
to be arriving. If they're not in the bushes already.

Boggis, half squatted behind the hearse, knew of the
action rather later, the door being hidden from him. He
heard the sound of feet on stone steps, the crunch of
gravel; and huddled himself closer in as the rear doors
were opened and the vehicle shook a little on its springs
when the coffin slid in on the rollers. Nobody looked
round the side of the hearse, nobody spoke. The gravel-
crunch receded, the feet went up the steps again; and the
thoughts of Sergeant Boggis almost exactly paralleled
those of Inspector Rosher. Wait. See who else comes
out—hope they haven't got guns.

The three coffin-carriers came back into the hall just as
Charlie came with Bernie along that passage beside the
stairs where Sir Roland dropped dead, each bearing a
picture: one a Corot, the other by Masaccio (active
1401—1428).

Charlie said: 'I left my shooter upstairs. When I
changed.'

Not like Charlie, to leave things lying around.

Certainly not a loaded shooter.

But Leonard offered no reproof. He said: 'Get it, Horsehead. Don't hang about.'

'On the bed,' Charlie said. 'Right beside the old man.'

Up the stairs went Horsehead, no longer needed down here now that the muscle-work was done. Charlie and Bernie turned again to fetch two more pictures from the cellar—a Constable and the earlier of the two Turners—as Leonard snapped to Ollie: 'Cop hold of them bags.' Himself carrying two, he led the jellified gardener out to the hearse again; where Boggis, hearing them coming, crouched closer yet to the black, beautifully maintained coachwork.

No blame should be levelled at this officer if only now was he thinking—until their arrival deflected him—that he ought to check, to see whether the two sets of ignition keys had been left in. Because if they had, the thing to do was remove them. All right—level blame if you must. We are none of us perfect, and to creep up and down opening and closing doors of the vehicle you are using as cover is not necessarily wise. To approach the limousine was, at this moment, out of the question. So Sergeant Boggis crouched with indrawn breath as two pairs of feet scrunched again over the gravel, and after a few moments retreated. Which is when the matter blew up suddenly in everybody's face.

A simple twig caused it. That, and the pumping of adrenalin that sharpens hearing and keys the body for instant reaction. The twig lay on the ground, among the roses. Rosher, moving a foot, snapped it under his thick-soled, boxy-toed shoe. Even to him, the report sounded abnormally loud. He saw the heads of the two men mounting the steps turn sharply; and feeling that leap of supercharged blood, said to himself: That's torn it. And without further thought he came to his feet, shouting loudly:

'Hold it!'

He was right to do it. No sense in crouching there now. Force their attention this way, hope that Boggis would up and take them from the rear. Pray that he was over there.

But Boggis couldn't see what was happening; and what did happen happened all in a few seconds.

Ollie, already well gone in fear, froze with his mouth open as a gorilla in durable blue serge and a black hat rose up with a loud cry from his well-tended hybrid teas. But Leonard, no bullets in his pistol, nevertheless dragged it from the pocket of his black suit and levelled it as three things happened simultaneously.

The gorilla sprang forward, caught on a rose-bush, swore, tugged free and came on, just as Boggis moved, and Horsehead came out from the house, carrying the only loaded revolver. It had to be Horsehead, of all the possibles.

That half-second's check while Rosher ripped himself out of the Dorothy Perkins may have made all the difference between relatively peaceful arrest and general mayhem; because without it, the inspector would have belted Leonard—question not his physical courage, he'd have gone unarmed at howitzers once the blood was up in him—before Boggis got to where he could see what was going on. As it was, the sergeant shot out from cover to see the gorilla-man moving, a pistol pointing at him point-blank.

The true wonder, under God, is not that a man will lay down his life for his friend, but that when all the chips go down with a crash he will hazard himself for a man not friend at all. Detested, even. Boggis had no cause to love Rosher. You could say that he hated him. And yet, in that flashing moment when he saw him jumping at a gun—and neither of the coppers knew it was unloaded—he didn't hesitate. To draw the fire, he roared: 'Oy!!' Just that. And he started forward.

Leonard had no time to turn before Rosher's mighty hammer—a bunch of bananas that made of the man Police All-England Heavyweight Champion three years running—felled him; but Horsehead was out from the door now. The punchy. The unpredictable, all filled with adrenalin and seeing his leader fall.

Doubtful, really, if he meant to pull the trigger. A lifelong fighting man, most likely his fists tried to bunch, by instinct. He was no marksman anyway, and a Webley is not all that easy to aim and hit with. But he managed it. Oh—surely by accident? The gun barked. Speeding Boggis spun, and fell, and lay still; and Rosher closed with Horsehead, hammer on the move again.

This was a mistake. Although, of course, it had to be done; and a man in sudden action works according to his compulsive nature. But to close with Horsehead was seldom wise. Rosher was trained in unarmed combat, and an outstanding amateur boxer in the days of his green salad; but Horsehead was a hard-case pro.

The hammer went home. The huge man didn't so much as blink. Confused, punchy, leaderless now and panicking, he, too, obeyed instinct. Somehow, Rosher's solid body rose into the air and the black hat jammed right down over his eyes as he flew head first into one of the stone porch-pillars and descended with a crash. He also lay still; as with a kind of sobbing moan Horsehead rushed past the paralysed Ollie and made for the hearse, flinging away the revolver as he went.

Four seconds only all this took, if that. Two policemen down, one called PC Wargrave racing forward now, over the lawn from the bushes where he had been left. Inside the house, Charlie and Bernie dropping the paintings they were carrying—the other Turner and a little Watteau—and rushing for the back door. Out front again, the huge, confused Horsehead, sobbing as he raced for the hearse; the man Ollie, down on his knees now, crying: 'Not me! Not me! Not me!'—God knows what he meant by it—and Leonard, up on his feet again. The hammer fist, unleashed off-balance, had missed the point of the jaw. Took him on the cheekbone. Stunned him, put him down; but not for the full count. He scrambled up, gun flown into the bushes, and started running.

By now Horsehead was in the hearse, fumbling for the ignition key. Leonard headed that way. He might have made it, too, might have scrambled into the passenger's seat; but Boggis was stirring now, thinking: Christ—I'm shot—I'm shot. And as good policemen will, not even knowing if they are dying or whether, if currently they are not, the action will result in guns barking again to blow the doubt away, he reched out to grab Leonard's ankle as it went by. So he got Leonard's other foot when, after a second's hopping, that man cried: 'Leggo—leggo,' and kicked him in the temple. Boggis sagged; lay still again as Leonard rushed on, shouting: 'Wait—wait for me!'

Horsehead might have waited, had he been in any condition to appraise the situation; but his at the best of times was not an analytical brain. He heard shouting; but PC Wargrave, too, was shouting as he raced across the lawn. So the big man, sobbing, let in the clutch with a bang. The hearse jerked into motion; and Leonard, also sobbing by now, made his last, despairing mistake. He leaped, grabbing at a coffin roller, to hang on at the back.

He is a good undertaker, Mr Sugden, and he keeps his gear in beautiful condition. His rollers are well oiled. No funeral party approves a squeaking and skriking as the coffin comes out. It came out now quite silently, and very swiftly, as powerful acceleration shot the hearse down the drive; trapping Leonard's hands just as they grabbed the back roller.

If only he'd had time to get his feet on to the rear step,

he'd have been all right. Could have ducked right down, doubled up as the coffin slid overhead. But he was still running when that terrible weight of oak-encased loot hit him in the face and went on; forcing his head back—and back—until his neck snapped. He died babbling 'O my Christ—O my Christ,' with his feet trailing. He never knew when the coffin finally cleared the hearse and the last roller, releasing his hands and breaking his back as it fell, spilling tomfoolery all over and pinning him to the gravel.

Oh, it was all so unnecessary. Damn—if they'd given up quietly, they'd only have done another spell of porridge. But Horsehead fired that shot; and now he was going hell for leather down the drive, while inside the house Charlie and Bernie, skirts hoicked up, had reached the back door; from where, through the window, they saw a copper. It was one of those days, obviously, when people get hooked up on things, because he was struggling to free his uniform jacket from a thorn bush.

Bernie, by this time, was in blind terror, what with shouts and a shot and all. He gabbled: 'They're at the back—they're at the back—they've got us—'

Panic is contagious. Charlie, even now, did not succumb entirely; but a deal of it brushed off on to him. He should have watched for a moment, to see what was happening out there; but Bernie's gibbering reinforced his mental image of a copper behind every bush. Even so, he was still thinking in some kind. No way out at the front, no way out at the back. 'Come on,' he said, and raced for the cellar, Bernie with his hat gone all askew treading on his heels.

There was only one man out back, and he as harmless as a rookie can be. Rosher's young driver; crouched in the bushes behind the house, as ordered; sprung to his feet in alarm and tingling excitement when shot came and shouting started, wondering what he was supposed to do.

Hooked himself straightaway to a thorn bush and couldn't get free, his own brand of panic tangling him ever more securely as he swore and struggled and wrenched. Absorbed, he never even saw the two faces appear at the window and vanish again.

Not bad thinking, Charlie's, considering the pressures upon him; but incomplete. The cellar gained, he bundled babbling Bernie down the steps into that marvellously constructed cavity and followed him, pausing to reach up and shove hard at the counter-balanced stone. The thick, ponderous slab moved easily; and nobody coming down into the cellar would ever have suspected that any part of that floor or wall was made to open.

Horsehead, about now, cleared the drive; seeing just in time as he got to the gates that a right turn would smash him into Rosher's car, parked in the middle of the road as block. He wrenched the wheel, shooting away to his left; and do not think a Daimler hearse can't travel. If it normally doesn't, this is merely because decorum abhors the racing gear-change and arrival at graveside in a shriek of burning rubber, everybody's eyes popped out. The big Daimler engine can go, though; so Horsehead was moving fast when he shot round a bend and found in front of him a squad car, travelling as fast the other way.

Here came the first of the reinforcements arriving from this end. The driver clung tight to his wheel; his oppo raised his arms before his face and said: 'Jesus.'

Don't worry, they weren't hurt. All they suffered was a slight jolt from a glancing blow. Sobbing still—the poor bugger could have stopped before this, and run off through the woods; nobody there to grab him— Horsehead swung the wheel left; bumped the police car; lost control and went smack into a tree. Shot through the shattering windscreen and lay draped along the crumpled bonnet, pumping blood all over his hired black. Still wore his top-hat, concertinaed now like a comedian's after it has been sat on.

In Sir Roland's cunning vault, Charlie said: 'We're all right here, they won't tumble it in a hurry. We're all right here, we'll get out when they've gone.'

'We can't get out,' babbled Bernie. 'We can't get out. Oh Jesus—oh Jesus—there ain't no mechanism down here. You shouldn't have—you shouldn't have—'

'What? What?' Charlie scrabbled his hands over the wall beside the steps; mounted them, to shove at the slab above.

'You'll never move it—you'll never move it,' wept Bernie. 'Oh Jesus—oh Jesus—oh Jesus—'

Perfectly right, nobody can move that slab from the vault.

At the precise second when Charlie began to scrabble and Horsehead went into the tree, Detective-Inspector Rosher stirred on the porch, fought his way to his knees and thought that he was blind. He reached up to rub his eyes and found the black hat crushed down over them. So he gripped the brim on both sides with square, fur-backed hands and levered upward. The hat came off almost with a hearable plop, and he saw, distinctly double, Ollie sitting on the bottom step with his hands covering his face, weeping; Leonard's body from the waist down lying in the drive, top half covered by coffin; and nearer to the steps the still and silent Sergeant Boggis, on his back now with a uniform jacket under his head. Beside him in shirt-sleeves stood PC Wally Wargrave, commanding an ambulance. And don't fart about, he said to his walkie-talkie. Get it here in a hurry.

Detective-Inspector Rosher addressed one of the two Wargraves. 'Where—where—what—where's . . . ?' Lights were flashing about in his head.

Pc Wargrave came over. 'Take it easy,' he said. 'Don't get up—there's an ambulance on the way.'

Rosher wanted to tell him he was all right, he'd beat the count, he'd be out for the next round. Then something of memory came. He pointed to Boggis; mumbled: 'Look after him—good man. Good man. I'm all right—look after him.' And he fell flat on his face again.

CHAPTER 14

It was a week before Inspector Rosher's vision singled out. Ten days before he was discharged from hospital. And he was the one who came lucky out of it. Three weeks went by before Sergeant Boggis finally butted the Dark Angel in the belly and fought his way back to where he was allowed visitors; and still, at this time, they were wondering whether Horsehead, all stitched and cross-hatched, would emerge eventually from coma or die in it.

The first visitor to be ushered in to Sergeant Boggis was Mrs Boggis. She deserved priority, having rushed to be with him as soon as the radio news bulletin shocked her ears and even her mother's. Through all the days since and all the nights she had been within call, torn with remorse and harrowed by guilt; because commonly, when one of a quarrelling marriage falls into great trouble, the other finds love believed dead is suddenly very much alive; and they grieve for their share in its smirching. So when she came in to the small room where he lay alone, annexe to the public ward, her cheeks were drawn and her eyes red.

She said: 'Hallo, Reg.'

He looked up at her. Some weight he'd lost, and he wore a bandage round his head. Cut it on the edge of a step, when he went down. Big graze, too, on his forehead, where Leonard's footwear homed. 'Hullo, love,' he said;

and because tears were suddenly running down her pale
face: 'Don't cry. It's all right—don't cry.'

'I can't help it,' she said. 'I can't—Sorry. Daft, really.
I'm—very happy, really. I meant to be all—happy.'

'I'll tell you what you are,' he said. 'You're bloody
lovely. Oh—you're bloody lovely.'

And now she wept in earnest. 'Oh, oh, oh,' she said.
'Oh, I'm such a fool. I've been such a fool.'

'No—no—don't,' he said in an agony. 'Oh
Christ—don't. You're lovely—I love you—I'm the fool.
I've been the bloody fool.'

So they spent the entire five minutes allowed by a
steely-sweet ward sister refuting each other's claims to the
greater foolishness and claiming it for themselves. And
when the sister appeared to put an end to it all, and
tactfully vanished while they said goodbye, he grinned
and said: 'Nip into bed, quick.'

'What, now?' She took on the modest smirk English-
women assume when, very gladly, they know themselves
lusted after.

'Don't hang about,' he said. 'You've given me a terrible
horn.' Which is frank and honest enough. Although, of
course, an intake of transfused blood does that, all on its
own. But the condition is exacerbated no end by an
uprush of love.

When she made that modest-maiden smile, which she
did very nicely although no maiden these seven years (no,
eight; there was a travelling grocer before Boggis), a
soupçon of dimple showed in her left cheek. 'You'll be
lucky,' she told him; and melting for him all the time.

'Wouldn't be much good anyway, unless you did all the
work. Can't feel a thing from the waist down. Except
that.'

'They say it'll pass off, though,' she said. 'They say the
paralysis ought to pass off.' They said it *might* pass off.
Don't hope for too much, is what they said.

'It'd better.' He grinned up at her. 'Can't even waggle my bum. Bugger off, now. Let me practise.'

At the door she turned. 'Oh—Mother sends her love.'

His grin widened. 'Tell the old bat to get knotted.' He said it lovingly.

She came again next morning; but today she had to wait while a rather precious young man in a pearl-grey suit asked him, for the benefit of a television camera set up by the bed, what he had *thought* about when he thought he was about to be shot dead. Then he asked him again because the cameraman said the light wasn't right. Then the sister came in to say they must go now, she couldn't have them overtaxing him; so they did a shot of her saying smilingly that he was the perfect patient, which taxed him for another ten minutes, five while she titivated, all flustered, and five for the shot. After which, discovering Mrs Boggis, they sat her by the bed to hold his hand while the precious young man asked her how it felt to be married to a hero, and what she *thought* about when she thought he'd been shot dead. Then they went away; and the sister, recovering suddenly, bustled her out and shut the door firmly.

The next morning, he being stronger, she shared visiting-time with the Chief Constable, Sergeant Barney Dancey (that good man who forced geraniums and brought him one in a pot) and various pressmen and odd bodies like PC Wally Wargrave, who popped in as everybody left and was promptly popped out again by the sister. She had just declared the session closed.

The next day was better. Somebody had realized she ought to be considered, so they had a little time alone. He was quite cockahoop. Policemen, like normal human beings, like to be hero, and he was thoroughly enjoying it. Still horny, he told her, but couldn't get a waggle out of his bum. Oy—the Chief had been very encouraging. Hinted there might be promotion in it. Ah—you're lovely. You're lovely. Here—put your hand under the blanket. Don't be daft—nobody's going to come in. Of course it won't hurt me—does you the world of good. Ah—that's nice. That's nice. Oh—hallo, Sister. Just talking to the wife.

Rosher came in during the afternoon. Well out of visiting-time, while the watchful sister was away for a cup of tea. When a skull takes a right whack they check it at intervals for some time after, and Rosher's had just been checked by a Pakistani gentleman who tocked his knees with a little rubber hammer and shone lights into his eyes. He did other things, too, and when they were done pronounced himself satisfied. Rosher went down one floor in the lift, and walked along to where Boggis lay. He knew where it was. Had wandered along once or twice since the sergeant left the intensive care unit, but they wouldn't let him in.

The inspector, of course, as other hero involved, was sharing kudos with the one who got shot. If his portion was rather less rich, this was because the public enjoys more the copper shot than one who merely gets knocked cold, by fist or cudgel. But television featured him, and newspapers snapped him ('Jesus Christ,' said one well-known editor, when the prints arrived on his desk, 'what are we running, a sodding zoo page?') and colleagues from the Old Man down were congratulatory. Press stories were bumped up a little by reference to his recent arrest of Frederick Sydney Lugge, awaiting trial for the murder of Sir Roland Goyt's maid. So everything was going along rather nicely. But he was not thinking about these things when he appeared at the annexe room door and said:

'Ha. Hmm. There you are, then.'

'Ah,' said Sergeant Boggis. 'Ah. It's you. Come in.'

Rosher advanced. He had intended to do it smiling, flourishing the bonhomie proper to policemen visiting a colleague mashed up in the course of duty; only the smile got stuck, somehow. He came with his beige eye-teeth showing, but the effect was not really bonhomous. 'Thought I'd just drop in,' he said.

'Ah. Very nice. How's the bonce?' When they told Boggis, after he woke up, what happened to Leonard and Horsehead, they told him also about Rosher's cracked pate. What a good job he landed on his head, he said. Might have hurt himself, otherwise.

'Fine. I've just been for a check-up. Fine. Thought I'd just drop in.' That's twice, the inspector thought, I've said that. He stood with his black hat gripped between his hands.

'Well—sit down,' said Sergeant Boggis. 'Help yourself to a grape. Every other bugger does.'

Inspector Rosher sat, on the little chair beside the bed. 'How're you coming along?' He still could not get the smile working. If anything, it was stiffening. But still the dogged teeth hung out.

'Fine. Great.' The sergeant spoke buoyantly. He *felt* buoyant. All was well. He *did* love her, she *did* love him. It wasn't all a crippling mess, their marriage. When he got out of here—oh, it would all be different. The way it used to be. 'I'm a bit buggered from the waist down. You know—no feeling.' What there is is a private matter, between her and me. 'They reckon it'll pass. The bullet nicked the spine.' Went right through. Very nearly got the heart.

'Good. That's good. Hrrrmph.' Now the smile had set hard. Rosher found it well-nigh impossible—always had—to express thanks. 'I—er—I reckon I owe you. The—er—he'd have blown my bloody head off.' Leonard's gun, the automatic he pointed at Rosher, had been found unloaded; but Horsehead might have unleashed at him, had Boggis not shouted.

'Oh—that's all right. Any time.' Very difficult.

Uplifted on his new euphoria, Boggis looked properly on the man they called Old Blubbergut for the first time. He saw, beyond the bombast, a gauche and awkward reserve, a basic—insecurity? He saw the difficulty with which the simian features clung to the brown-toothed grin; and he thought, with a small shock:

Poor old sod. He's old. A year, and he goes for scrap. And all on his tod, no domestic life at all to help him when it comes. Poor old sod.

He said: 'We nailed 'em, though, didn't we? What was the gear worth, do you know? The papers say it runs into millions. Pictures and all.'

'It's still being sorted out,' said Rosher.

Now the sister appeared. She came with a rush, told by a probationer as she sipped her tea that a big man had gone in to Sergeant Boggis. She said: 'I'm sorry—I can't have this. No more visitors until morning.'

'It's all right, Sister,' Boggis said. 'I feel fine. But for this gentleman, I wouldn't be here.' Now what did he mean by that? That shouting for Rosher's sake put him in; or that Rosher's immediate launching of himself at Horsehead prevented a second shot that might have blown him away into eternity?

'I'm sorry, but you are not all right. You've had more than enough for one day.' No sweetening in the steel now, the lady bristled her hackles at Rosher. 'I must ask you to leave.'

'Ah. Hrrmph.' Meekly—meekly!—Rosher got up. Out from his pocket came the dreaded handkerchief, one of many turned crumpled and grey-white since his fat wife went home to mother. 'Sorry, Sister,' he said. 'Sorry.' And he blew a trump that jerked her bolt upright, one hand flown to a rather over-starched left bosom. Even Boggis, who knew what was coming, started in his bed, and a nurse going by with a sample dropped the bottle and skipped lively, trying to dodge the splashes.

Rosher mopped up as he went to the door; where he turned, and coughed, and said: 'Er—about that other business.'

'Other business?' said Boggis.

'In—er—your house.'

'Oh. Yes.'

'I—er—I wasn't . . . I—er—didn't . . . Hrrmph.'

'It's all right,' said Boggis. Of course he didn't. Would she have let him, poor old sod? Not likely. He, Boggis, must have been bloody mad to think it. An old, sad gorilla. 'It's all right—I know.'

'Ah,' said Rosher. 'Hrrrmph. Well—be lucky.' He tramped away.

Turning to plump up his pillow and to tug straight bedclothes already straight, Sister administered to Boggis a little scolding; which he took with a broad grin. All lifted up, he was, in a kind of second-time first love. As was Mrs Boggis, going about her housewifely business. Neither of them knew, as yet, that two people basically misallied do not come via over-emotional reunion into lifelong fairyland. Sooner or later, the euphoria dies. But for now, Boggis lay back in his bed and felt for lone Rosher the sincere but patronizing pity felt for the life-battered loser by those who believe they have it made.

CHAPTER 15

Horsehead might have told the police enough to start them on a thorough brick-by-brick search of the house, looking for Charlie and Bernie. There are several reasons why he did not.

One was his addle-pate condition, not at all modified by smashing that pate through a laminated windscreen. Another: he was a good pro in his way, and loyal to the

code. He took it into his muddled mind that they had won
clear; so he kept his mouth shut. Didn't even mention the
cellar. When a man like Horsehead goes dumb, nature
gives him a head start. Well, it made no real difference.
They'd have been dead long before the month was up
during which he lay very nearly dead himself, hooked up
to glittering machines, stitched plain and purl and in
coma. From which he emerged at about the time when
Boggis went for his first outing in a wheelchair.

Ollie might have told, too; but Ollie was gone
completely. Utterly blank and withdrawn. Not even fit to
plead. Familiar pattern, the psychiatrists said. The mind
subjected to too much stress retires. He is still in
Rampton, detained at Her Majesty's pleasure. Not that
she ever goes near the place. Unless she slips in incognito
now and again, to enjoy a jolly good laugh.

The problem from the police point of view during that
month while Ollie crouched silent and Horsehead lay
unconscious, was that although very obviously other
villains were involved, nobody knew how many or who
they were. The undertaking group, one of whom
eventually wriggled free, had seen only two men, the dead
one and Horsehead, they opined; and Mrs Rummidge
only one, which scared her so much she could give no
description at all. But the young reporter—he got a
wonderful career boost out of it—said he heard several
voices, and he was there before the hearse arrived.

There was a brouhaha, the young man's syndicated
sensationalism saw to that; but who, exactly, was being
sought? Boggis mentioned seeing Charlie Palkin with the
man Hardcastle; and Charlie had vanished, so he'd be
one. But who else? By the time they sorted it
out—Bernie's landlord eventually reported him as a
missing person—they were long gone. The police (and
Horsehead) believed, under and out and overseas. They
are still listed as missing, wanted for questioning.

On a sweltering day of high summer, Boggis in court and walking now with crutches (becoming a trifle irked, too, by the tender ministrations of his wife), Horsehead stood trial all alone. Pleaded guilty. He'll be an old man before he gets out. Expressed regret from the dock, and privately when the policeman went to see him, for the shooting of Sergeant Boggis. Didn't say a blind word about cracking Rosher's skull. Clammed up tight about every other matter, too, which didn't help him a bit; until he got to Dartmoor, where his fellow inmates greeted his arrival with clapping, and treat him to this day with enormous respect. Incidentally, the police dropped one charge against him: that of being concerned in causing the death of Sir Roland's nephew. Well, they couldn't have made it stick, he wasn't even there. They didn't need it, anyway.

Freddie Lugge's ill luck continued, exacerbated by his sheer funk and normal ineptness. Once you become entangled in a mesh of fear, of course, whatever cool judgement you may possess goes flittering through the window; and Freddie never had much to begin with.

Brooding alone in a remand cell, the imaginative mind sets in a diminishing vicious circle. Fear adds to fear. And fear is weakness, is loss of all self-reliance. In criminal circles, it leads to desperate trust placed in the untrustworthy.

Thus: when Freddie heard of Leonard's death it brought a kick of relief. It removed one horrible threat. He decided now was the time to reveal all; but here he paid the penalty for consorting with bent but clever solicitors.

Mr Marks wanted out. He did not relish its being made public that he handled the affairs, not only of Freddie, but of Leonard, Charlie, Bernie and all; plus many another such. Much gelt came to him through dubious

channels; and there wasn't much of that in Freddie. To
further complicate his position: all the other Mr Markses,
and Mr Spencer, were discreet and honest men. They
wouldn't enjoy it, his being connected on the wrong side
to two related and highly publicized cases.

So he gave very doubtful advice. He said: 'If I were you,
I'd keep my mouth shut. Their case isn't all that strong,
bit of luck you might get off. Or you might just cop
eighteen months for manslaughter.'

'I didn't do it,' Freddie said.

Mr Marks waved him down. 'Yes, yes, yes. So keep your
lip buttoned. You don't want to find yourself done for
accessory in a copper shooting. They'll throw the bloody
book, for that one. The law comes very heavy on copper
shooting.'

'They couldn't do that,' Freddie yapped. 'I wasn't even
there.'

No honest lawyer would have made the following
statement. Freddie had the right of it. Doubtful if
anybody could pin an accessory charge on him. If they
tried, a good lawyer would have put up a heck of a fight.
But Mr Marks said: 'Don't you believe it, son. They don't
bother with the rule-book when a copper gets shot. And
then there's this nephew geezer—causing his death.
They'll clap that on top. Believe me, they're going to
come down heavy. They've got to—look at the publicity
the press is giving it. And the bloody copper's paralysed.
That's going to weigh.'

Clever. He knew his man, he knew what remand can
do. He knew a Freddie, frightened and without friends,
will cling to his lawyer as a child clings to a father. Will
trust him. Freddie went into court a week later than
Horsehead; answering to the murder charge and
vehemently pleading not guilty

And still his bad luck held. He had to get, on the jury,
two very persuasive ladies; one middle-aged victim of a

man in a similar line of business, who had robbed her of her all; the other a roaring Lesbian who hated all men on principle and the lady's man in particular.

His counsel tried hard. He went for the obvious weakness in the case against his client—and there were Percy, Rosher and Boggis all in court, Percy representing the police. It was completely out of character, he said. Mr Lugge had no history of violence. And a man with his looks and admitted sexual experience has no need to rape or savage plain little orphan chambermaids. His word, that.

Here is a warning: when you declare love for ageing ladies and vanish with their savings, be sure you stay vanished. They may swallow the financial loss; but Hell hath, indeed, no fury like a woman when a man has rogered her, and stood in her poor, lonely dreams beside her at the altar, and scarpered; leaving her alone again, feeling old and undermined and facing a bleak future with a new hate and no money.

So the prosecution pointed to handsome Neville Heath; and more damning, produced statements from ladies who knew Freddie in the past, and when they saw his picture on telly or in the papers, leaped spitting to swear to anything—anything—that would destroy him. Violence? Certainly. Any particular kind? Sadist, he was. Since two of these ladies never reported him to the police from sheer humiliation, he could not even claim that they were swearing false witness because he robbed them. In view of the general ambience, it wouldn't have counted much for him had he tried. And his counsel knew it.

Then there was the judge. Mr Justice Ganworthy. And here, Freddie's luck really set him up. On the night before Mr Ganworthy tried Freddie, his well-beloved youngest daughter was chased down a dark alley by a man who certainly did not intend to offer her a milk shake. She escaped with nothing worse than a bad fright, thanks to a swift kick while she delivered, with commendable presence of mind and splendid accuracy, straight to the goolies; but it soured Mr Ganworthy's outlook. His summing up came very close to directing the jury. Subtly, because he knew his law; but definitely.

This is not to say that official rigging took place. The job of the prosecution is to prosecute, and judges are only human. As are juries. Alas, poor Freddie.

On a misty morning in late summer, when Sergeant Boggis was down to a stick and a limp—fed to the teeth with idleness and beginning, from sheer frustration, to spar again with his wife—Detective-Inspector Rosher happened to be in an official car, driving by the end of that lane leading to Notley House. The radio spoke. Somebody just rang the station, to report trespassers in the grounds, digging up shrubs and things.

Yes. Near to transplanting time, you see, and enough of the stuff would fetch a fair profit, flogged to a street-market trader. Look at the price of roses, these days.

Young herberts. They'd be young herberts. Rosher reached for the microphone. 'Inspector Rosher,' he said. 'Car Eff-seven. I'm close—I'll have a look at it.' He was here, really, only to get away for a while from the universally detested paperwork. Decided to move up the day an interview planned for later. Grabbed a car and went for a ride. Had no objection whatever to any diversion that prolonged it.

They were indeed young herberts. No more than thirteen, fourteen years old; perhaps put up to it, perhaps operating on their own, gathering greenery as they would gather anything left unguarded; hoping to flog, if the market was not there waiting; or ready to dump and pass on to other matters if no quick-cash buyer turned up. They took to their heels as Rosher's car came through the gates, brandishing plants and whooping as they fled towards the back of the house and the wall they must scramble over before they scattered in the woods. Rosher recognized one of them, promising son of a regular client who specialized in stealing cars.

He made no serious chase. That lad, at least, would be brought in soon, on some other caper if not this. An eye kept cocked towards his father's garden might be a good idea, get the bugger for receiving. Right up his nose, that'd get, he'd lam hell out of the little sod. Not for nicking, but for attracting police attention. It appealed to the inspector's sense of humour. Yes—he'd have a word with whoever covered the beat. For now—take it easy. Have a look round, see if they've broken in anywhere or vandalized anything.

They seemed not to have done. Perhaps he arrived too soon. A few greenhouse panes were shattered, but this is to be expected when a place is left unattended for months on end. By now, weeds grew among unkempt grass where Ollie once kept a wonderful smoothness. The grounds were taking on a shaggy look, the blind-eyed house an air of drab depression. Rosher stood in the drive and looked about.

Over there, where the lads had dug roses out and laid them by for transporting away, he very nearly met his death. That was where Boggis lay, and the corpse of Leonard almost here, he supposed, about where he was standing. He didn't know, he'd been too dizzy to sort it all out. Strange, how little remained of violence afterwards, at the scene where it happened. You'd never think this place had ever known more than the backfire of a motor-mower on the lawn. He could have used that motor-mower, but somebody nicked it, and all the gardening tools, almost before the ambulances and squad cars turned right out of the gates.

I'd like to know, he said to himself, *what happened to the other buggers. And who they were. Don't tell me that*

*mad gardener geezer wasn't coerced. Probably had a gun
on him all the way, but he's gone round the twist so he's
no help. Boggis's old client Palkin—he'd be one. And
how many more of 'em—skated through the shrubbery
and over the wall while my young twat had his back to the
house, all tied up in a hawthorn bush? Coppers? Don't
make me bloody laugh. Gets up your nostrils, the thought
of 'em away somewhere and laughing at you, when you
might have had' em all, dead easy.*

*Mind you—there could have been a lot of shooting,
and we'd had no time to arm anybody. No firm reason to,
either. More than Boggis might have got it.*

He crossed the drive. They'd rooted out the roses where
he crouched. There they lay, bundled up. Nothing here
but holes, scattered dirt. Footprints, and an object all
covered with wet earth beside the hole that must have
held the bush he'd used as cover.

Idly, he turned the object over with his foot. His eyes
snapped to attention. 'Bloody hell,' he said.

Detective Chief Superintendent (Percy) Fillimore was
back to work by now. Had been for months, favouring his
back but otherwise fully fit, if you except his stomach and
the normal small ills his hypochondria insisted the flesh
was heir to. Today, suffering no more than the start of a
cold he hoped would not turn to pneumonia, he was
sitting in his office ticking papers, initialling them and
putting them into his out tray, when knuckles knocked his
door. 'Come in,' he snapped. Not because he meant to,
but he had a narrow voice shaped that way.

It was Inspector Rosher. Alfred Stanley Rosher,
carrying in his hairy hands an object resting on a plastic
sheet. 'Thought you'd better have a look at this,' he said
brusquely; and dumped the object on the desk.

Percy looked at it, with distaste. 'What is it?' he
snapped. None of the snap left his voice when his visitor

turned out to be Rosher. Be sure of it.

'Handbag. Black plastic with gold-plated clasp. These were in it.' The inspector proffered a small bag. One of the miniature sacks into which police put the odd bits and pieces of personal belongings that come to them.

Contrast in hands here, fit for Dürer. That big, furry one, holding out the bag; a narrow, white and blue-veined, thin-fingered one taking it. Percy shook the contents on to his desk. One lipstick, a little small change, one lacy handkerchief, one compact; two toffees and a small, unframed photograph. Rosher's thick finger jabbed as Percy studied it. 'That's Eva Brewster. The kid who was murdered.'

'Where did you get this?'

'Up at the Goyt place. Kids pinching plants, they unearthed it. Buried under a rose-bush.'

That's all he needed to say. Percy was no fool. You don't find chief superintendents inflicted with lolling heads and tongues that hang out. Whatever the man Lugge did, it wasn't likely that he crept up to Notley House to bury her handbag under a rose-bush. Not that night, not later. But a gardener. With a beard. Engaged already, perhaps, on spring digging in that bed . . .

In Percy's stomach the nervous tic began. 'Ah,' he said. 'Better let Forensic—'

'Forensic's seen it. No dabs outside, too much mud and rain. Been underground too long. Nothing. One on the inside, under the flap. Belongs to Hardcastle. The gardener.'

Percy sat in silence for a moment. Then he said: 'I think we'd better take it upstairs.'

Out came the inspector's handkerchief. Percy braced. When the racket died away, through his mopping up Rosher said:

'Uh-huh. I think we had.'

They left the office and began to mount the stairs to

the Chief Constable's room, square feet and narrow feet, Percy carrying the handbag. Half way up his waltzing stomach backfired with a report that rivalled Rosher's famous trump. He didn't even say pardon.